Farewell to Love and Other Misunderstandings

Studies in Austrian Literature, Culture and Thought

Translation Series

Herbert Eisenreich

FAREWELL TO LOVE

AND

OTHER MISUNDERSTANDINGS

Translated and with an Afterword

by

Renate Latimer

ARIADNE PRESS

Library of Congress Cataloging-in-Publication Data

Eisenreich, Herbert, 1925-
    [Short stories. English. Selections]
    Farewell to love and other misunderstandings / Herbert
Eisenreich: translated and with an afterword by Renate Latimer.
          p.   cm. -- (Studies in Austrian literature, culture,
and thought. Translation series)
    ISBN 0-929497-57-0
    I. Title. II. Series
PT2665.I8S313   1993
833'.914--dc20   92-2232
                                                                 CIP

Translated from the German:
Twenty-two selections from *Ein schöner Sieg* and
Die blaue Distel der Romantik ©Verlag Styria, Graz/Wien/Köln
and
"Erlebnis wie bei Dostojewski," "Abschied zur Liebe,"
"Die neuere (glücklichere) Jungfrau von Orléans," "Wie einst, Lili
Marlen" ©by Christine Fritsch, Vienna. All rights reserved.

Cover design:
Art Director: George McGinnis; Designer: Rod Andrada

Copyright ©1993
by Ariadne Press
270 Goins Court
Riverside, CA 92507

All rights reserved.
No part of this publication may be reproduced or transmitted
in any form or by any means without formal permission.
Printed in the United States of America.
ISBN 0-929497-57-0

Contents

A Dostoevskian Experience 1
Farewell to Love 17
The Newer (Happier) Maid of Orleans 29
The Blessing of a Bad Reputation 37
The Naked Truth 43
A Nice Victory 49
"Wie einst, Lili Marlen" 51
A Misunderstanding 61
A Friend of the Family 67
Life After Death 87
A Successful Surprise 94
Consequences of Garrulousness 96
Failed Revenge 97
Love's Labor's Lost 99
The Blue Thistle of Romanticism 102
The Fall 106
A Detour to Happiness 110
To Die and Yet to Live 111
A Divine Judgment, of Sorts 113
Punt E Mes 119
In Praise of Craftsmanship 135
A Portrait of Man and Wife 141
A Case of Self-Conversion 148
An Unexpected Reunion 152
Lust and Lasciviousness of Monogamy 154
Between the Lines 156
Afterword 165

Acknowledgements

I wish to express special thanks to the Europäisches Übersetzer Kollegium in Straalen, the Humanities Development Fund of Auburn University, and to Christine Fritsch in Vienna.

Renate Latimer

"A Farewell to Love," which appeared in *Short Story International*, No. 61 (April 1987), and "A Friend of the Family," which was published in *Short Story International*, No. 68 (June 1988), are reprinted by permission of International Cultural Exchange, Great Neck, NY.

"A Dostoevskian Experience," ©1984 by Loyola University, New Orleans and "The Blessings of a Bad Reputation," ©1991 by Loyola University, New Orleans are reprinted by permission of the *New Orleans Review*.

A Dostoevskian Experience

She came from a wealthy family, had married into an equally wealthy one, and was now living with her husband and children half an hour's drive outside the city in a two-story country house by a lake, living in a rhythm of veritable affluence that had been handed down for generations. She cultivated her mind and spirit through the daily reading of great authors, at present primarily the Russians, and she trained her body in various athletic activities which the spacious grounds behind the house and the lake in front so generously permitted. She devoted herself lovingly to the education of her children, and was her husband's most affectionate friend and most loyal advisor, keen and agile. And although coddled by nature and her milieu, she never lacked that proud modesty, heedful of moderation, which so conspicuously distinguishes the wealthy from the merely moneyed, though the latter's accounts may be greater. Thus whenever she went into the city once a week to acquire this or that for her personal need, she seldom took the car, although her very own, even with chauffeur, stood at her disposal, but rather she preferred the single-line railway between her town and the city, which transported workers, clerks and older pupils as well as those who were leaving the country for the city for business reasons or for pleasure—attending the theater or a concert or merely a dance club. In the train, of course, as was her due, she chose a first-class compartment.

Thus she had also taken the train this time. In the morning she had paid a visit to her husband's city office, had delivered his instructions, had perused the latest correspondence, and had dined at Spitzer's with the two gentlemen who had been employed to look after her husband's far-reaching business dealings. She took her leave, strolled through the heart of the city, tried in vain to telephone an old friend from mutual boarding-school days, a very famous (and justifiably so, according to the opinion of the experts) singer at the opera. Then she visited her tailor, instructed him to measure her for a winter coat, handled a variety of fabrics, felt and wrinkled them, had this or that bolt lifted into a daylight which, already very subdued—as if filtered a hundred times by the indolent, satiated autumn air—fell through the panes of the show window into the dusky room lit by neon lamps. Walking on, swept along by the strollers of the late afternoon, she gazed into shop windows along the streets between the Cathedral and the Stock Exchange until it was time for the hairdresser's. And when she left the salon one hour later, after the procedure was finished, she felt the damp and cold autumn air creeping from her neck and temples under her lightened hair. A few blocks further on, in one of those large stores where working-class women buy electric trains and true-to-film Indian costumes for their brood, she purchased a game of tiddlywinks for her children, made another attempt, and yet again in vain, to telephone her friend the singer, and finally landed, as was so often the case on these quite aimless walks, at the shop of the old antique dealer, a sensitive businessman with the manners of a charming gentleman, who had furnished her boudoir and had also delivered many a precious trifle to her house. And there she discovered, with the hardly necessary gentle assistance of the antiquarian, who indeed was sufficiently acquainted with her taste, a Japanese tea set of very delicate and doubtless old workmanship which would be greatly appreciated by her husband, who had been born in Japan and for almost two decades there had cleverly managed and multiplied the wealth acquired by his family in the Far East trade. And now in Europe he was regarded as one of the most remarkable experts of that part of the world, so that it was not merely on account of his cuisine and cellars that cabinet ministers and bankers and diplomats liked to dine with him; consuls and industrialists appeared at tea, and military attachés invited him to morning flights over the mountains. His wife thus discovered this tea set which would please him enormously, especially since he had lost many personal items of remembrances from his Japanese years during the chaos of war. Meanwhile reflecting upon all this, she hesitated on account of the not at all commonplace price. Eight hundred marks: that was a good deal of money for someone accustomed to handling money. And finally she decided against the purchase and said that she would think it over.

She stepped outside into the street where the late autumn evening damply descended among the dully-brooding houses like a clammy drizzle suspended in the air. A solid crape of mourning floated down from the low sky, gathered before the timidly lit windows and coiled itself around the street lamps. The abrupt contrast of manifold varieties of forms, the densely packed colorful diversity inside the antiquariat and the rough masses dissolving in the fog, blurred contours out here in the street—this contrast made her shudder and shiver. Involuntarily raising her shoulders to her chin, she stopped and stood still. Because she had not, after all, acquired the tea set, she felt as if she had lowered herself into a more humble milieu. And suddenly she felt miserable, exceedingly miserable, and reprimanded herself for having been petty, stingy, uncharitable; and in her thoughts she already turned back in order to return to the antiquarian. Meanwhile as if rooted she stood there. It seemed all too embarrassing to her to inform him already of her change of mind. She would prefer to write him in a few days or telephone him or, best of all, wait until her next visit to the city in a week ("Well, I have thought it over, I'll take it . . ."). But the misery, the void, which meanwhile hollowed her body, which had overtaken her entire being like an emptiness, so that she believed everything would collapse inwardly within her, this miserable vacuum did not permit itself to be filled with arguments, with deliberations, with mentally planned reparations. And now she was more than irresolute: deeply helpless she stood there, a mummified discomfort in front of the gate of the shop, which the proprietor had closed again (taking a last measured bow, turning about-face while retaining a stiffened spine), whereby the soft clicking sound of the snapping lock had abruptly erased from her hearing the gentle, Christmasy chime which resounded as if from a music box during the closing and opening of the door. Immobile she stood there, paralyzed in her soul and incapable of turning her steps toward the train station, incapable of going home, now that her city visit had obviously ended. As if she had to be ashamed and fear that her shame could be discovered at home, her shameful behavior could be read in her eyes like the headlines in the evening paper. However to reenter the shop once again: for that too she lacked all strength. Thus she stood without a will, totally overwhelmed—as if by immovable gravity—by the sensation that no matter what she would now undertake, would be inappropriate, embarrassing and shameful for her, unworthy of her, no matter how she might turn it.

At that instant she heard beside her a whispering voice, a mere breath, as close as if it were speaking into her ear: "Please, would you give me some money—only for a little bread?!" With relieved agility she turned her head and noticed a young woman's face narrowly framed by a dark blue scarf, and she realized that it was raining, that it must have been raining for some minutes: several curls had protruded from under the girl's scarf and were clinging wetly to her white forehead, and these curls glowed darkly with dampness, and little pearls of water sat on the girl's brows, and still others below the eyes on her downy cheeks so that it appeared as if tears had flowed down. And she felt the dampness in her own face. She looked at the girl, still held the girl's softly and hastily spoken sentence in her ear (as if it were rotating there) and remembered that she had not eaten anything since noon and that it was the hunger which had dug a hole in her into which she felt she was plunging—yes, the hunger and nothing more! Yet before this thought, completed to be sure, yet by no means proven in its correctness, could have developed into a complete proof, other thoughts arose, burying the first one. She reflected: "Now, yes now, I have the opportunity! The opportunity to recover in a roundabout way what she had just forfeited in the antiquarian's shop; and at the same time the opportunity not to have to return home immediately, while her humiliation had not yet been completely eradicated." And she kept thinking: "And what an experience! Not merely to have it tangible before one, but to act, to participate personally, to be involved in something that she had never experienced but had only read about until now, in a Dostoevskian experience!" And shadowlike another thought flashed past: how enthusiastic her friend the opera singer would be when she was told about it! And to the girl she said: "You know what, why don't you come and eat with me? I'll invite you to a nice restaurant!" And she thought: "No, not to Spitzer, that is too elegant, she could be embarrassed; presumably she is wearing nothing but a cheap dress under what's left of this coat. Regina too is not appropriate, yes, the train station restaurant would be best. There one eats well and not too expensively and without being conspicuous in any way!"

The girl breathed: "For God's sake, no!" She stared, as if she had been most dreadfully propositioned, into the face of the strange lady whom she had dared to address—this tall, beautiful woman with the voice, the natural intonation of a sister. The woman meanwhile had already beckoned a taxi, directed the girl towards it with a mild pressure on her upper arm, guided her into it, instructed the driver with two words which the girl could not understand in the interior of the car, then sat down beside her and said: "You are not to be embarrassed at all, you are simply my guest tonight!" And when the girl seemed to try to utter an objection, less with her mouth than with her entire thinly-hunched body: "Really, you don't need to apologize, you don't need to explain anything to me, that's how life can be; but please be nice now and do me the pleasure of dining with me!" And she felt tempted to place her arm around the girl's bony, angular shoulders; but then she thought that such a gesture, even if it should succeed in all its unprejudiced cordiality, could intimidate the girl even more rather than free her from her intimidation. And she desisted. She continued to think that it would be a priceless pity if, on account of impatient, even if best-intentioned, carelessness, she would prematurely frighten away this rare, precious catch, which fortunate chance drove straight into her arms. At once, however, she sensed such a train of thought as a roaming in forbidden realms and said, in order to bring herself back to the right path: "Let's just have a leisurely meal together, the two of us?"

The girl realized that the driver was taking the direction of the train station toward which she had been hastening from home for some time, hesitating, deeply ashamed, before every woman she felt bold enough to address (and then failed to do so after all) and she thought that the closer they came to the train station the more favorable her chances would be. And as she deliberated, as if rummaging with feverish fingers in her brain, when and above all how she should make her situation clear to the woman, the driver already turned, as he had been instructed, toward the train station square, made a sweeping curve, approached and pulled up under the protective roof above the sidewalk in front of the ticket hall. Behind the threads of rain on the car windows the girl stared outside like a prisoner behind bars. "Drive up to the restaurant!" There the driver stopped the car, jumped out, flung open the car door, accepted the fare, and let his purse containing change quickly vanish in the pocket of his wind jacket after the woman's gesture indicated that the sum was correct. The girl thought that the moment had now come to explain herself. But meanwhile she already felt a gentle touch, irresistible, on her arm: her hostess had taken her arm and was already leading her up the stairs to the restaurant, inside and across the room to one of the few free tables in front of the large windows which offered a view upon the platforms and train tracks below, where several trains stood ready to depart. "But now we want to enjoy a leisurely evening, don't we?" The girl, who hitherto had not said a word, still did not say anything, took off neither her scarf nor her coat, stared down upon the platforms beneath whose flat, gently sloping roofs with rain gutters she could see several suitcases, and in the most restricted space, the quick legs but, due to the visual angle, not the faces of waiting travelers. "Why don't you take off your coat, Miss—!" The girl thought: "Oh no, no, no!" At the same time she reached under her chin where her scarf had been knotted, loosened and lifted it from her hair, and hung it over the back of the chair. And thought: "Oh, if only she weren't so damnably kind—how am I supposed to be able to tell her?!" She felt incapable of disappointing her benefactor, of revealing everything to her like the contents of a bag full of stolen goods. She now took off her rain-damp coat, particularly since the strange lady was assisting her, and let herself resignedly be pressed into the positioned chair. "We had best drink a brandy first, that will warm us up." And when the girl was still silent: "Surely you do like a brandy?"

"No," the girl began hesitatingly, with lowered eyes, softly and full of nausea at the thought of drinking. However when she realized that brandy would give her the courage, which she now needed to undo the error she had committed on account of the strange lady's kindness, the courage which she now needed as never before in her life: "All right, please, if you suppose so, ma'am?"

"You see!" the lady said, satisfied with her first successful inroad into the silent, virtually walled-up being facing her. And she ordered the brandies from the waiter who was just bringing two menus to their table. "French brandy, please!" And she turned again to the girl: "But please don't call me ma'am again; simply call me by my name!" And she told her her name. And thought: "What a pretty girl! Not at all a bad face, a dull face! God only knows how she has sunk so low?! Perhaps someone is ill at home or she herself may be ill! Likable, but exceedingly intimidated! Probably begging for the first time—and I, I can perhaps change it so that this first time may also be the last time. I'd only have to know what is really the matter with her! But she'll tell me her story, no doubt she'll definitely do that!"

The waiter brought the brandies. "The ladies have decided?"

"In two minutes!" The waiter retreated. She raised her glass, smiled encouragingly at the girl. The girl groped for the glass, raised it to her mouth, took a sip, sipped again and then with a violently-angular gesture drained the glass. Her deep breathing delineated the constriction of her throat, she brought her head forward again, suddenly suspended the motion with a glance at the clock on the wall, actually only the white wall with twelve black lines and forty-eight black dots in between and two black hands encircling them, and she thought: "There are less than ten minutes remaining, yet still enough time to run through the entire train, to look into every compartment!" And she thought: "If I don't say it now it will be too late!" And she said: "I would like—I would like to tell you something—," and overwhelmed for the second time by her own boldness, she lost her painstakingly controlled language which turned into such a confused, tormented stuttering resembling weeping that the lady interrupted her gently and said, "Let's just eat first very quietly; after a good meal it's much easier to talk—yes, it's much easier. Why don't you make a selection!" She pushed the opened menu in front of her lowered face. "Would you like a veal cutlet with a salad?" The girl nodded barely perceptibly with the inert, uncomprehending submission of one whose death sentence has just been pronounced. "Or do you prefer stuffed peppers with rice? . . . And this too would be delicious: ragout with fried potatoes!" And since the girl continued to nod automatically, she waved to the waiter and ordered two ragouts with fried potatoes and a small decanter of wine, and for the girl another brandy before the meal. She would have liked to tell the girl something cheerful but the words that came to her mind felt insipid as soon as she formulated them mentally. Thus she too was silent. Outside in front of the window the locomotives were puffing indolently into the foggy evening, and individual lights, green, red, blue and white lights, were swimming in the damp darkness. The waiter brought the brandy, but the girl did not touch it. At the surrounding tables more and more people took a seat, mostly travelers who had chosen a night train and were now eating their evening meal before departure. But there were also people here from the city who had come to the restaurant merely for the sake of eating. Trains were called out, the reluctantly articulated clearing of the throat of a railway official on duty, workers' trains into the immediate vicinity, and then the through-train "with special railway carriage to Le Havre." The girl heard the announcement crackling and rustling, stared at the white wall with the black lines and dots and hands as if her gaze could bring the time to a standstill, realized that this was her last chance, and was silent—as if an enormous guilt were sewing up her mouth. Still unaware, yet surmising with a certainty transcending all awareness, that not the request itself addressed barely half an hour before to the strange woman had devoured all her energies, but rather that the small untruthfulness of this request had totally and completely drained the vessel of her will, which barely half an hour ago had seemed inexhaustible to her. The waiter brought the dinners and poured the wine into the glasses. "And now," said her hostess, "don't think of anything but your meal!" Awkwardly, as if with stiffly frozen fingers from which all blood has been drained, the girl took her knife and fork into her hands, started to cut and then let her barely raised arms sink again feebly. And she was thinking, while the other half of her thoughts was striving toward only one so near yet oh so unattainable goal, that she sat here imprisoned, caught in a trap, whose casing was constructed of her untruthful request, and whose little door, closed shut behind her, consisted of the immoderate fulfillment of that request! "One must not press her, one must let her very slowly become herself again," the woman thought meanwhile, and began to eat as inconspicuously as possible. Suddenly, however, she let her knife and fork sink as she saw the girl's gaze, a petrified convulsed face, aimed beyond her in deathlike rigidity. She turned around, as if perceiving behind her back a suddenly loud danger, but only saw the white wall with its black clock there. Down below, from the direction of the tracks, a whistle cut through the stillness that hovered whisperingly over the entire train station. Then a locomotive started to pant, puffed violently and short of breath, and gradually found its rhythm that paralleled the droning grind of the wheels. The girl remained immobile, bursting with tension. No, her hostess thought, she is so very intimidated that it's best to leave her alone! She searched for a name-card in her purse, added three folded bills, slid the little package under the edge of the girl's plate, and said, gathering all the warmth and cordiality at her disposal into her voice: "I am just realizing that it's already very late for me." And withdrawing her hand, as if after a discovered theft: "Honestly I don't want to offend you! I only would like to help you, insofar as I can. Please write to me, I have influential friends, I am quite certain that we will find something for you!" And rising: "Do me the favor and pay for everything and don't say another word about the rest, all right?" It was not until now that the girl noticed the name-card and the three ten mark bills, touched them with trembling fingers, raised her head and then suddenly it burst forth from the enraged face, a darting flame of disappointment and despair: "Now, now, now!" She swept the money and the name-card from the table, jumped up, tore her coat from the hook and rushed outside, past the unobtrusively astonished waiter and the nearby tables where the people were craning and twisting their necks and staring after the girl and then looked back to the so abruptly abandoned woman who was quickly paying the waiter. And someone at the neighboring table said, and said it so loudly that she had to hear it: "Of course, she made demands on the girl!" She gathered her belongings together and with lowered head she walked away, still considering whether she should not have taken the scarf, which the girl had left lying on the chair, as a concrete remembrance of this unmastered adventure. And just as she abruptly rejected this fleeting thought, the waiter surfaced beside her and handed her the scarf. Simply to avoid any further complications she accepted it wordlessly. And she hurried toward her platform where, she knew, the next commuter train had to be departing very soon. And after she had extinguished the light in the compartment, she sank back into the cushions. The girl, meanwhile, rushed across the train station square, retracing the way she had driven in the taxi, in her numb mind nothing but thoughts of him, whom she had come to see just one more time, one last time, and who had now departed without her having been able to see him and tell him that it was not her fault alone, by God in heaven, not her fault alone! This last letter too her father had intercepted because he could not stand him, this "foreign fop," this "visage from overseas," or simply because he did not want to give up the daughter who brought home the money for drink. And today when by mere chance her father's intoxication had more quickly than usual turned into a rattling sleep, and a letter informing her of his final departure fell into her trembling hands after all, it was too late or still not quite too late if only she had had the money, the twenty-five pfennigs for the streetcar and the ten pfennigs for the platform ticket. But these thirty-five pfennigs she had not had, and even if she had succeeded in shaking her father awake he would sooner have beaten her to death with his emptied bottles than given her the money, no matter for what purpose, and there was no one in the vicinity from whom she could have borrowed the money. Thus she had hurried away on foot, had then addressed the beautiful stranger and thereby all had been lost. She had not been able to free herself from the dilemma, that consisted on the one hand of her untruthful request and on the other hand of the immoderate fulfillment of this request, had not been able to free herself in order to admit the truth, this simple, little, oh how comprehensible truth: that she still had to see him, him, him, to see him, but no longer to hold him, but simply to explain to him how all had come about between them, to tell him all this before he rode away, so far away that she could not even imagine it, and never to return—yes, to tell him how all came about between them and indeed no longer to hold him, not to persuade him to turn back, but merely to explain everything to him, and with this knowledge to bury the discord and grief and resentment which henceforth would separate them more deeply than the deepest ocean between them—if only she could succeed in still seeing him, in telling him all, in offering him a good word and receiving in turn a good word from him: so that, if all should come to an end here, it would not end other than the way it should have lasted! She had addressed the woman, the beautiful stranger, with the request for money for a little bread, because it had seemed to her that bread was the only thing on earth of comprehensible value to men and its lack was felt so tangibly that men were ready and capable to become enraged on account of it, and therefore perhaps also to help. And now all had turned out to be much better and therefore much worse! She was simply caught and had not been able to disentangle herself from this abused helpfulness to which she had appealed out of helplessness with an elusive word such as "bread." And she was caught, trapped between her own tiny lie and the excessive kindness of that beautiful, tall, wealthy stranger—who was now sitting in the rumbling train and thinking. Thinking that it must have been the hunger which had gradually hollowed her out, had made her miserable and had made her susceptible to adventures which her nature could not master. And that things had only been able to come this far because in the antique dealer's shop she did not immediately do what she would now have to make up for tomorrow on the telephone. ("Yes, well, I have thought about it and have slept on the matter; I'll take it . . . .") In spite of everything, she did not feel happy at the thought of the tea set, and the more tenaciously she clung to this thought the more painfully betrayed she felt by the actual booty of her roaming in uncertain territory. Wasted time, wasted money, wasted effort, senselessly and uselessly squandered kindness, and finally the humiliation! Never, as far back as she recalled, had she failed so completely in anything without being able to find an explanation for the failure or a blame in herself. Her heart and her head were overwhelmed by the question as to what had actually happened and why she had been unable to master this adventure, since truly she had not spared time, money or effort and had done her very best possible. Thus she strayed from irritation into annoyance, from doubt into indifference, from shame into the desire to forget. She saw herself helplessly at the mercy of the new experience of blameless failure, she did not know how to deal with it, she wanted to rid herself of it. As well as rid herself of the girl's scarf. So as if nothing, nothing at all had happened, and therefore nothing, not even the scarf should remind her of anything! She searched for the scarf in her purse in order to place it in the baggage rack opposite her. And as her fingertips touched the coarse woolen fabric in whose shabby texture a trace of dampness still remained, she felt once again as she touched this small pitiful piece of reality that had stayed with her the entire indestructible reality of the evening's encounter, this encounter with the thin, pale girl in the drizzle in front of the antiquarian's gate. She felt with the indubitable certainty of all her senses and transcending thoughts that she had met not merely any poor and wretched creature from that half of the world unfamiliar to her, but rather the incomprehensible fate of a human being which makes that being—more than any poverty or any misery—pitiable, since not even goodness, even if all the means of the material world were at its disposal, is always and necessarily capable of helping, of healing, of saving. And she also felt that experiences such as the one into which she had been swept do not simply let themselves be cast aside in forgetfulness like a strange scarf in the baggage rack. And finally she felt that the more intimately her fingers became acquainted with the object of her touch, the purer the sorrow streamed from this touch, as a kind of solution to all that had happened in reality, the sorrow of all true experience which she had believed one only makes with the fingertips of the soul: the sorrow into which she now sank, descending to the primary cause of life, precisely where this sorrow, as it bores its shaft into the depth, suddenly changes upon impact into the incomprehensible fortitude thanks to which man returns, ascends and lives. She had wanted to help, and it was she who had been greatly helped! And as the train came to a stop in her hometown, she wept without restraint into the coarse woolen scarf of the girl, wept and knew that at home her tears would be noticed, but continued to weep softly and finally silently on the way home, at home, in bed and into sleep, into a new day, into a new life where she found herself again with empty hands, yet all the richer.

Farewell to Love

The three months were over. He had finished the job late into the afternoon yesterday, had completed it just in time, and now in three hours his flight would depart and carry him to another place on this earth, where another job would have to be done. Actually he wanted to eat some lunch before leaving, but he was not at all hungry now. He walked about in the room and gathered his belongings which had accumulated during the past two months that he had been with her or had stayed with her. It had been about two months since he first had been with her; no, it must have been longer, probably two and a half months. He had not lived in this city alone for very long, and she had not hesitated for very long. "Good God," she had said, "I am not, after all, a saint." It was not until now that he remembered these words. He had not loved her, definitely not. He had merely felt comfortable with her: not much different from the comfort offered by a fur coat in the winter or a lukewarm shower in the summer. He had felt the desire to hold her in his arms, or not necessarily her, simply something soft, gentle, vibrating, which made him in turn feel harder, stronger, more secure than he actually was. And she had just happened to cross his path. By chance it was she; it could have been any one else. He had never once mentioned love. He had exercised control over himself, out of curiosity, to see how this word could be avoided. He had told her: "You are so wonderfully young," and "How well we do get along," and "All the women I meet make me think of you, because none could be as sweet as you," and similar things. However, never the word *love*, because it was not love. He felt very comfortable and she, too, felt the same. She had never let him doubt that, proving it with her little shrill cries that assaulted his eardrums, hard and round like pebbles. But it had definitely not been love.

And now he gathered his belongings which had accumulated these past two and a half months. He had spent the night with her. She had to go to work at eight and therefore had left him the keys. He still lay in bed for awhile and sipped the tea (already cold by now) which was left over from breakfast, then took a long bath and dressed slowly. He had, after all, nothing more to do. His hotel bill was paid, his suitcases there had been packed the day before, a company car would transport them to the airport, and he had brought only his traveling bag with him. From the bag he now took out the microscope. He had remembered, just in time, that she, a physician, would surely be able to use a microscope. And so he had bought it yesterday. And now he was here alone, walked back and forth in the room for the last time, from one corner to another, diagonally, and tried to step in such a way as to avoid the seams of the floor-covering. He was annoyed that today of all days she had no opportunity whatsoever to get away for one hour for lunch. "I have worked there for less than four months, and I simply can't afford to run off during working hours just to have lunch with you," she had told him. And then she also had added: "I am so terribly sorry. I would have loved to take you to the airport." And he had interrupted her and had said: "To the train station, perhaps. But at the airport it is horribly boring. Even for the traveler, and especially for the person who is saying good-bye. One can't even wave. One should go to the airport only to pick someone up." He noticed that she was about to make a reply—but said nothing and merely went into the bath and then returned with darker lips and paler cheeks. No: it suited him quite well that she couldn't come to the airport because he hated to see clear and clean things, as this affair with her had been, end in wordless waiting, or perhaps, and with some women one could never be certain, see this affair dampened by tears, fade and finally be obliterated. However, that she couldn't even spare a little time to have lunch with him—that had completely destroyed his appetite. After all, there were enough physicians at the clinic. And he continued to look for his belongings.

Here was a flashlight that belonged to him. There was his cigarette lighter. Here was the flat traveling flask filled with cognac. Here was the long-stemmed straight pipe (the English call it a churchwarden) which he had smoked in the evenings, in fact, just yesterday. And in the closet hung the sweater he had worn here, and the three ties were also hanging there. They were hanging across the shoulder of her winter coat. And on the bottom of the closet between her pullovers and blouses lay a worn shirt of his. And as he took his belongings he felt like a thief. He stuffed the sweater, ties, and shirt, into his bag, his house slippers and pajamas as well, and then took everything out again to fold it carefully. And then he remembered the handkerchief which he used to place under the pillow, and as he bent over the pillow he caught a whiff of the scent of her hair. She had always resisted a little when he had lifted her splendid hair from the nape of her neck—perhaps due to the birthmark (half the size of a fingernail) on her left side. And one evening, he now recalled, he found her with short hair, completely swept up from her neck. Next to the bed, which during the day folded back into a couch, stood a wobbly little table with an octagonal top. The table wobbled because it was collapsible, like those folding chairs which deer-hunters take along on hunts. Such things could infuriate him tremendously. Whenever the table wobbled, and it wobbled at the slightest touch, he asked himself when, after all, would one be obliged to fold the little table and press it under one's arm? It was a very attractive little table, its collapsible divided top decorated with inlaid work. At present it was concealed by the breakfast tray with the teapot and the two cups, the sugar bowl, the plates and the egg cups (all the dishes were in iridescent green), a little bread basket lined with a white, gold-edged napkin from which protruded that little tube of pills for stomach indigestion, which some time ago, she had brought him. "A physicians's sample, therefore free of charge," she had said and smiled. But probably she had bought it. As he reached for the little tube, the table wobbled, but he wasn't much irritated this time. For a split second he was even thinking of carrying the tray into the kitchen, but then he didn't do it after all and went into the bath. And on the counter below the mirror he noticed now, as if for the first time, all the jars and tubes and cans and little bottles which she was using. And from among all these jars and tubes and cans and little bottles he picked out his toothbrush, his shaving lotion, his nail file and his comb. And from the window sill he took his electric shaver and here too was her comb, and next to it a tuft of her hair. And then he stared for some time at all these pale-green and pink items on the counter, with white and gold and black in between, by Inka and Yardley, by Helena Rubinstein and Jobrun. And he stared at the hairspray and nail polish and eyebrow liner and mascara, at all the creams and lotions and tonics and powders with their magical names like "Mysticum" and "Beauty Milk" and "Eau de Lanvin" and "Crema Brilla" and "Fond-Fluid," at all this almost embarrassing foreign arsenal of beauty care, which surely could not serve beauty but rather more directly serve self-assertion. He, in any case, had never known a single woman who had looked as beautiful after the make-up procedure as before. It served a cult which he had secretly resented. This arsenal, however, with its pale, delicate colors now made the room all the more intimate for him. The room which he now reentered contained the same colors: the floor-covering made of pale-gray synthetics, the pink Biedermeier wall paper, the curtains' deeper shade of green, the white sheets with the virtually invisible green stripes, the red bedcover, which still hung folded across the back of a chair before the small, dainty desk. The desk was of white lacquer but the edges and curves were trimmed with gold, and some of these golden decorations had discolored and turned brown or peeled off. One saw the naked wood resembling scars. On the desk top, on the left, were stacks of books, pharmaceutical leaflets, notes, newspapers and magazines of all sorts, and gray and green folders, and on the very top of the pile a tiny ashtray of pink porcelain containing a tiny burnt match, but no ashes and cigarette butt. And now he recalled that she had come back to the desk, already wearing her hat and coat, and was holding a burning cigarette in her hand. And then she had left the room, very quickly and without saying a word. From the bed his eyes had followed her out. On the left rear side stood a telephone, in the middle a desk lamp with a green shade, and on the right a flat drawer in which she stored letters and bills. Near the right front there were more piles of books and pads and folders, and in the front center, in an area not much larger than a sheet of paper, lay notes and pencils and scissors, a bone letter-opener and a few vials, two packages of cigarettes torn open, a postcard depicting a dense forest with a church steeple, a key to a suitcase or a mailbox, and lots of other things. And in the midst of all this he found his fountain pen and address book. Last night he still had to make several telephone calls to the men with whom he had worked and also to the airline company. He took the two things belonging to him and adjusted and pushed the other items aside to make room in the center of the desk top for the microscope. And beneath the glass, which covered the top entirely and which was secured on the four corners by small golden-colored clamps, lay numerous newspaper clippings, actually headlines only: "Seamstress Stabs Her Husband," The Dead Man Leaves the Cathedral," and similar odd items. When he had first seen these he thought them a little silly. He did not approve of papering one's desk top or door or walls with newspaper clippings. But now he looked at them and read these texts as if they could reveal something to him. Some of the clippings were a bright white, and others faded and yellow, and three or four entirely brown, almost like wrapping paper, and only at the edges were these darker newspaper clippings. were a bright white. Some had round white circles with holes in the center. Evidently she had tacked these clippings to the wall in her student apartment. And as he pushed a pile of magazines aside to continue reading these texts, he found the earring which she had searched for this morning—in the bath, under the bed, and everywhere in the kitchen. And now he recalled that she had actually always searched for something: either for the monthly bus ticket or a glove or a certain book, and after awhile it had happened that it was he who always located the missing object. He dialed the number at the clinic, asked for her, and told her: "I have found your earring. It was lying on the desk and slipped under the papers. I'll place it in your jewelry box." And afterwards he didn't know what else to say, and when he hung up he still had quite a bit to say. But he only stared in front of him at the desk. On one of her note pads he read the word "lightbulb" written three times: on the first line it was written in her usual handwriting, beneath it on the second line in letters twice the size, and on the third line it was printed in capital letters. For a week now the lightbulb in the hall had been burned out and she had forgotten again and again to buy a new one. He took the key ring from the ceramic bowl standing on the little varnished table, went downstairs and bought a lightbulb. And upstairs he changed the bulb. Tonight she would not again have to be irritated by her forgetfulness, as she was yesterday. And for a moment he was quite cheerful. He threw the note into the wastepaper basket and then he carefully lifted the microscope from the black, velvety-red case and set it on the desk where he had cleared some space. He felt pitiable and shabby with this gift. She will be able to make good use of it as a physician, he had thought. And now he knew that she would be happier with the lightbulb.

And he knew that this microscope was no compensation for all that he was removing from the transformed apartment: his sunglasses, his city map, the package of scientific periodicals on the bookshelf, which he had bought on the way to her place and then had leafed through here. On the shelf beneath stood the record player, still open from last night, and on the turntable lay a record. He turned it on and lowered the arm; it was "Struttin' With Some Barbecue." "When I come home from the clinic in the evenings or early mornings I need, first of all, something invigorating," she had said. "Ten minutes of Satchmo and a schnapps, for example." And last night she had played a few records, and this one last. But the skipping melody pained him now. Perhaps it was too early in the day for it. And he raised the arm from the still turning record and stopped the turntable and took the record off and slipped it back into its cover and turned the stereo off and closed it. And on the bookshelf where the record album had lain, he now detected, next to a torn open double-package of hose, the book dealing with his field of specialty, which he once had lent her when she wanted to know more about what he was doing. And now he threw it into his bag and set out to erase every reminder of him and of his presence here. The room was supposed to be as it had been before him and seem as if nothing had changed. He shoved the bed linens into a drawer, pulled the cover over the bed, and adjusted the decorator pillows, and best of all he would have liked to pack the microscope again because his two and a half months here were supposed to be extinguished. Everything was supposed to be as before. Now he hung her morning robe in the closet and set the sewing basket in the little cabinet in the hall and on this little cabinet (among paper handkerchiefs, a scarf, and a burst bag of peanuts) lay his Hertz charge card. On weekends he had sometimes rented a car and had driven with her into the country to go swimming or to some rural inn. He drove very well but didn't actually enjoy driving. However, when she sat beside him, driving had been fun: he had felt like a child showing something to another child. That would change now. And he took the card and returned to the room and asked himself in amazement how it could have happened that his belongings, otherwise most carefully arranged and in order, could have fallen into such disarray, could have been devoured by her disorder. "Only he who knows order, knows what I shun," he had once written on a piece of paper and had placed this paper in the midst of the chaos on her desk. And she had read the small insolence like a love letter, with transfigured face, and folded the sheet and put it in her wallet between her photos. And he carried the breakfast tray into the kitchen, and in the kitchen on a shelf between glasses and spoons and empty cans and a spool of twine and a pot holder and a moldy lemon lay his pocket knife with the rinsed corkscrew. Last night they had drunk a bottle of wine, as they did every time he was here with her, and the knife had been here for several weeks because her corkscrew, a complicated gadget with all sorts of levers and wheels never worked properly. It was a Swiss army knife, brownish-red with the familiar white cross, the best pocket knife in the world, with several blades, with scissors and files, with a saw, a pipe cleaner, can and bottle opener, and a dozen other instruments. As he now took the knife and snapped the corkscrew back, he knew what he had been doing the past hour: he had plucked to pieces both of their hearts. With sharp-clawed fingers he had not merely seized his belongings from her, but himself from her. And in the room, like a thief almost, he hastily reached for the picture frame standing on the white-gold lacquered little desk, raised both of the glass panels with the photo and replaced the glass. And he reached for his portfolio and placed the photo next to the others. His briefcase contained the illustrations to a work dealing with the history of more recent fortifications, Berlin 1803. He had the book for a long time, but without the illustrated portfolio. He had found the portfolio here, in an antiquariat, on the way to her place. And here, together with her, he had leisurely studied the photos. In the center there was always depicted a colored view, surrounded (in dainty, separate little boxes) by floorplans, longitudinal and cross sections, architectural details and fortification projects. And he told her about Vauban and his first, second and third system, and about the typical Vauban assault, and about his Dutch opponent Coehoorn, and about Cormontaigne and Montalembert, about Speckle and the two Landsbergs. He spoke about escarps and counterscarps, about crenelated frontal façades and the tenaille structure, about Kaponieren and Courtinen, and she simply liked these photos. On the following day she bought a photo frame, and every time he came, this frame contained a different photo. And now the frame was empty and he did not know what to do with it. He looked at the microscope once more and then stared at the empty frame. He slid the portfolio into his bag, tore his coat from the hook, dropped the key ring off at the coffeeshop, pressed himself into a taxi and said: "To the airport, quickly." He knew that it took no more than thirty minutes to the airport. And he also knew that he still had one and a half hours until his departure: one and a half hours to turn back. He also knew that he would never come back here, just as he knew that he would never be set free again. He would forget her eyes, her face, her neck, the mounds of her breasts and the curve of her thighs, and lastly the scent of her hair. But never the white desk with its peeling golden edges, full of stacked books and papers left and right, and all the things in between, never the wobbly little table with its inlaid work on the divided, collapsible top, never the blouses and pullovers on the bottom of her closet, never the green on this floor and the other green of the curtains, never the burnt match in the pink ashtray, never the torn open double package of her hose on the bookshelf, and never any of this. And never the gaze into the empty frame. He knew that it was too late. Of course he could have changed his plans and stayed here at least another day. And then he could see. But it was too late after all this. After he had betrayed her: with her.

Somehow or other he had arrived at the airport and at his airplane. There were very few passengers, and he had a window seat. He looked outside and saw the terminal building gently gliding from his view, and not very distant from the runway, actually parallel to it, a high wire fence, and behind it a path. And there he saw a taxi coming to an abrupt halt, and a woman jumped out. She was not wearing a hat, only a coat, and the hem of a white gown showed beneath the coat. "I have worked there less than four months, and I simply can't afford to run off during working hours just to have lunch with you." Now he caught the words in his ear again. And she was running from the path to the fence and she was waving, and her other hand was clutching the railing, and she waved, as if to stop the airplane, and then, at last, like someone who knows that no one is even looking back. And then her arm sank down and her hand remained hanging beside her other hand on the fence, and she stood there behind the wire fence like a prisoner. All that he saw. And then, as the airplane swung around toward the runway, the land receded as if someone was pulling through his gaze an endlessly long, colorful cloth whose colors were already fading. He saw it already only as washed-out and blurred, and the stewardess asked him if something was the matter. "No, no thanks. Not really. Perhaps I had a little speck of dust or something like that in my eye." And as the airplane ascended, he turned to the now empty window and for two or three seconds he pressed his handkerchief against his eye.

The Newer (Happier) Maid of Orleans

Not only the officers of the garrison but pretty much all of the so-called society of our little town had already wiped their mouth on her. To be sure she only had one at a time but in the course of the years it added up. She didn't even derive much pleasure presumably from the thing itself; she simply found it chic to fall out of bourgeois bounds and into everyone's bed. Admittedly, she was an attractive presence and especially by our small-town concepts a decidedly extravagant one: boyishly slender and so tall that her bobbed hair towered above everyone; no other girl tangoed and shimmied and danced the Charleston as well as she did, and she is said to have been the first woman in the whole town to appear in public with red lacquered fingernails; and of course she smoked, very heavily in fact. She had been engaged officially at least three times: at first to a lieutenant from the Dragoons, who had brought back from the war a gallery of medals, which were softly jingling when he bent over the billiard table in the "Casino Café"; then to a merchant's son, whose father had just been elected to the Parliament; and lastly to a student, who had been quite a bit younger than she, but already divorced and earning his money during vacations as a technical assistant in the paper factory. But at thirty she still had not yet found a husband, and at thirty-five she no longer was desirable at all: beneath the powder and rouge her skin had yellowed, her eyes stood like murky pools between swollen lids, the formerly so defiantly curved lips had narrowed to a shriveled, sometimes bloodless bursting scar, and her hips had thickened, whereas the muscles of her arms and legs vanished and the bones protruded angularly; there was something rattling about her gait as if she were dragging a sabre across the pavement.

Around this time Hitler was marching into Austria, and when he rode through our little town in his open automobile he happened to press her hand, which she, among all the other rejoicing people along the street, extended toward him. Her subsequent behavior was often attributed to this handshake; in truth, however, the matter was very different: Toward the end of the twenties when she no longer went with the Dragoon lieutenant and not yet with the son of the Parliamentarian, a young man had tried to win her favor, but, because he lisped, had been ignominiously rejected. During this winter, this particular man had surfaced again, as an army officer, had approached her and finally asked her for a rendezvous at the "Westbahn Inn," as popular as ever with the military. In the room upstairs he let her undress, lured her and then shoved her, after she had already lain down, in front of the big mirror built into the closet door, and said, while intentionally letting his tongue protrude between his rows of teeth: "With this revolting sack of fat and bones I am supposed to go to bed?" Almost simultaneously he pulled open the door and from the closet there emerged an elderly, ragged peddler who hadn't shaved in three days and probably not washed in three weeks; and pointing to the stupidly grinning vagabond he added: "This may still be good enough for you—but not I, not any longer, not for over ten years already!" By the time he had spoken his last word he was outside already and locked the two inside with the room key which he had carefully kept ready. He had hoped for a minor scandal; but since the two prisoners were able to come to terms with the innkeeper who was concerned about his reputation, he himself had to spread the story everywhere, and he enjoyed doing so, because he was very proud of the fact that this joke had cost him a solid hundred (and that was, at the time, quite a bit of money). So the matter became public after all, and surely only for that reason—because in the cafés and dancing halls, in the dim hotel rooms and in the bushes down by the river she had certainly not let herself be told about politics—surely only for that reason she stood a few weeks later rejoicing along the street and let her hand be pressed, and surely only for that reason she forgot the tango and shimmy and the Charleston and wore her now longer hair in a bun and led a folk-dance group and undertook similar things which were in vogue at the time. She still understood nothing of politics, but she believed in that man who had pressed her hand, and no longer thought of all the men who did not sleep with her.

And something else occurred: she had removed her past as an actor removes his costume after the performance; nothing was left of it, nothing—except her smoking. When she had been young, it was always said: "A woman does not smoke," and still she had smoked, although in the beginning she always had to hide her nausea. Now it was said: "The German woman does not smoke," and now she could give it up even less, although she sometimes sensed her smoking as a secret disloyalty; and therefore all the more eagerly she displayed her loyalty where it could be seen by all: no longer merely in the folk-dance group, but also in the evening classes and in the courses in the "womanhood movement," whose local leader she had been designated, and finally in the aerial defense; for in the meantime the war had started. And with it of course also the rationing of all commodities, including cigarettes; and the distribution of these declined noticeably faster than that of bread and lard and meat. She gave food cards for tobacco cards, she exchanged small articles of value for cigarettes, paid foreign workers, who bargained with cigarettes, unhesitatingly every sum they demanded, made various attempts now and then with all sorts of teas and dried herbs, and at last longed for the long-promised final victory especially because she was certain that she would then once again have enough to smoke.

That's how it went from year to year until that very May, when the two fronts of the allies closed over the rest of Germany, as the blade of a pocket knife snaps into the haft. Vienna and Berlin were already in the hands of the Russians, and the Americans approached from the other side; and in our little town too we mobilized for battle: invalid officers trained the *Volkssturm*, women and girls dug foxholes and hideouts down by the river and at the town's edge, pioneers hung explosives on both bridges and prepared roadblocks, and field police tied captured deserters to trees along the main avenues; and everyone calculated repeatedly daily as to who would arrive earlier, the Russians or the Americans. And then suddenly the *Volkssturm* was sent home, the women and girls no longer had to dig, the explosives were thrown into the water, and no one was hung any more; because in the distance one heard now and then the cannons, and everyone rejoiced that it was not the Russians but the Americans who would arrive first, and soon. She, however, without a cigarette for one and a half days already—she was as deadly sick as she had been in the beginning when she started to smoke—she now saw the Germans deserting their (to be sure no longer alive) *Führer*, just as the men had at one time deserted her, and now suddenly she understood the true significance of that pressure of the hand: as a sealing of a like fate. She climbed into her training suit, as solidly and solemnly as a knight into his armor, and placed the air raid helmet on her head, whose hair she had combed for some time now in a man's style; and before the mirror of the hall wardrobe she examined her appearance for a long time: beneath the helmet her nose protruded like a bare bone.

In the Home for Hitler Youth she ran into half a dozen perplexed boys, and one of them, in his black-blue winter uniform with the swastika band, took her on his motorcycle, and in the depot of the *Volkssturm* they seized hand grenades and anti-tank grenade launchers, and beneath a sky in which the hostile planes were stirring like fish in the water, and between houses, from whose windows white sheets were waving, and past soldiers who no longer knew whether they were marching forward or backward between the fronts, and finally through a zone of total emptiness and stillness, where only burned-out cars and overturned cannons and scattered hand-weapons everywhere and equipment and uniform gear silently bespoke the waning war, she rode, four anti-tank grenade launchers pressed to her breast as a woman would otherwise clutch her child, she rode toward the Third U.S. Army. But at the sight of the approaching tanks, the boy was so startled that his motorcycle was flung out of the curve; he himself lay bleeding and his companion semi-unconscious in the meadow, while the head of a grenade launcher, which had been ignited during the fall of the motorcycle, rolled across the road hissing and howling. The tanks came to a halt; one of them pushed itself up the slope to have a view of the curve; then the three others took the curve and assumed a staggered formation. Several men in brown uniforms climbed out of the hatches carrying loaded pistols and one of them knocked the scattered grenade launchers and hand grenades with his foot into the road ditch, and another had a look at the unconscious boy and carefully wiped the blood, which had run out of his nose, from his face, and yet another planted himself before her and brandished the barrel of his weapon along her back and talked to her intensely; he wanted to find out something about German tanks and German soldiers, and she didn't quite understand him, she only turned around and sat up and finally rose, because she did not want to be shot while lying or sitting down. The American had smudges of dried motor oil on his face and hands, and he held his short carbine, with its barrel pointing down, as lightly as a whip, because he was a very tall, massive man. And although he looked totally different, she now thought, to be sure immeasurably briefly and evanescently—the thought was merely like one of those clouds which slightly dim, here and there, an otherwise blue sky, without actually becoming visible as a unique formation—she now thought of Carlo and the other Italians who had worked as prisoners in her father's small concern and to whom she had been so inexplicably attracted; and attracted all the more, the more she had been urged by her parents to avoid any association with them. And then suddenly, from one day to the next, the Italians no longer had been prisoners of war, and on this day when the prisoners too became normal human beings in her father's eyes, on this day, then, she had the courage to let the long dammed-up flood of her darkly thrusting emotions bubble forth before Carlo, with the overheated (because of the parental opposition) forthrightness of a fifteen-and-a-half-year-old; and Carlo had done what every other man would have done in his stead too, and then had handed her on to his comrades. And she, she had felt nothing more, could feel nothing else than the thought: "So, that's it? Nothing more than this?" And now when she thought the same—to be sure immeasurably briefly and evanescently—and simultaneously saw how the dull black barrel of the carbine raised itself, there emerged, like the smooth chestnut from its prickly hull, her defiantly girlish face from the murky features, and with tears of rage in the corners of her eyes she said: "Give me a cigarette at least!"

The American hesitated, then he saw his chance. He pushed back his helmet, offered her a whole package, and said she should come along behind the next bush. She went along, and smoked the while. And then another waited, and then yet another, five men occupy a "Sherman," there had been four tanks, and meanwhile several jeeps and trucks had arrived on the scene and a few more tanks, and then other combat units moved up, and then supply columns and staff and medical officers, and the word got around—she had moved to a nearby empty haystack in the meantime, she was also fed from time to time, and so during these few days—while the military commanders of Germany signed the document for capitulation first in Reims and then in Berlin; while the still living leaders of the regime hid in *Lederhosen* and behind black eye patches; while millions of German soldiers unbuckled and marched East and West into captivity; while millions of German civilians were beaten out of their property by the mob of the liberated countries; so during these few days she came into the possession of far more than a hundred packages, with which she then was able to survive the worst times.

The Blessing of a Bad Reputation

In our house, which had been hit by bombs during that fateful night and was gutted as far as the third floor, there lived twelve families. More precisely: there were nine families, two bachelors and one widow. We had all been living for quite some time in this house, and we all knew each other quite well. We saw each other after all not only on the staircase, in the courtyard, and in the communal laundry room, but also at the grocer's, in the tobacco shop, in the little pub across the street, on the way to church, and of course, as now, in the air-raid shelter. For over ten years no tenant had moved out and no new tenant had moved in, only the subletters at the widow Siegel's and at the Kowalskis changed from time to time. At the moment they happened to be an official in the Armed Forces and a war-disabled medical student at the widow's, and a machine knitter, who had been bombed out and whose husband was at the front, at the Kowalskis. During all these years only two deaths, one marriage, and three births had taken place: it was a truly quiet house with nothing but respectable tenants. And yet, although there was no cabaret dancer in our house and no hidden Jew, no one living in sin and no member of the Reichstag, not even a drunkard or a hysterical woman, nonetheless there was constantly a bit of investigating and snooping, a bit of meddling and gossiping going on. And actually only Fräulein Klara was totally ignored as an object of curiosity.

That changed, however, after the said night of bombing. The person on whom everyone's attention was now focused was a thoroughly honest, modest, pious being in her late forties, a picturebook maidservant, who had worked since time immemorial for Professor Bierich, an old bachelor on the fourth floor. She never performed her chores reluctantly nor spoke a word too enthusiastically. Even on Sundays her clothing remained unadorned, nor did it even intimate a body underneath: she was not a woman, she was simply Fräulein Klara. Moreover, she looked as if she were made entirely of the dust which she swept away daily in the Professor's apartment. And now suddenly everyone said: "Who could have imagined that of her?" And everyone replied: "Not me." Still others asked: "Do you really believe it?" And their reply was: "It's obvious that she had somebody upstairs, now that the Professor happens to be in Italy. And when the alarm sounded, she naturally didn't want him to go into the cellar with her. She didn't want to reveal her visitor's identity. A soldier no doubt." Others said: "Of course, we sensed it at once from her wailing and blubbering." And still others said: "And the fact that she still doesn't say anything is, of course, the best proof." (It also didn't occur to anyone that no one had actually questioned her.) Naturally the most absurd speculations abounded: for example, she and the Professor had had a secret child together and the charred bones were those of the child and not the earthly remains of her lover. These and similar conjectures, however, could not prevail for long against the general view that she had a soldier upstairs. Only the caretakers of the house, evidently out of professional vanity, opposed that view and retorted stubbornly: "It wouldn't have escaped us if she had taken somebody upstairs."

The main dissension among the residents concerned the question of how this affair was to be judged on moral and human grounds. The puritanical Noltes and the Armed Forces official damned such relationships on absolute principle: the former alluding to the already superabundant presence of immorality and the latter, an incredibly ugly human being of dwarfish proportions, probably acting only out of envy. The machine knitter was outraged that Fräulein Klara hadn't brought the man into the cellar, but the one-legged medical student reminded her that many soldiers at the front were instinctively reluctant to enter an air-raid shelter, and that it very well could have been the now-deceased person's own wish to remain upstairs. The couple named Günther, on the other hand, were visibly upset that this "dissolute person in a penitential frock" (Herr Günther's actual words to the widow Siegel) had always been held up as a role model to their only, and not particularly domestic, daughter. Frau Siegel, thereupon, was so amused that she spoke of it all over the house and neighborhood and finally revised her originally rather stern judgment of Fräulein Klara to a liberal one. And several others rejoiced more or less openly: some, because they saw their thesis strikingly confirmed—that there was no virtue involved, simply a lack of opportunity. Others rejoiced out of sincere sympathy: "Such a loyal, decent person—for her especially we should not begrudge the pleasure of also experiencing some moment of joy, even though it ended sadly." Thus the tenants spoke of Fräulein Klara, who walked untouched and unsuspecting in the midst of all these rumors and whisperings. Of course the gossip was fueled by the fact that the tenants had to live more closely together than ever before, on the undamaged stories of the house and in the cellar. As the tenants' judgments of Fräulein Klara changed, so did their relationships to her. She, of course, did not notice any change at first: that Frau Nolte still returned her greetings, but her words were more abrupt; that the young medical student treated her with as much consideration as he would a person grieving and bereft; that the machine knitter shared with her a letter from the front from her husband; that the caretakers eyed her suspiciously like a peddler; that the widow Siegel tried to engage her in conversation about her previous marriage; that, in short, they began to discern in this creature of dust a human being, a human being of a kind similar to themselves. That they discovered her soul.

And not merely her soul. Pühringer, the foreman, the bachelor from the erstwhile fifth floor, who had now taken up quarters with us down below, followed her with his eyes on the staircase, and henceforth he shaved every morning. And in the evenings when he came home and had washed himself, he put on a tie.

In the meantime the Professor, after receiving a telegram from Fräulein Klara, returned from Padua, where he had been undertaking historical studies, to view and register the damage. He turned to me in this matter and said: "You, as a lawyer, know more about this than I. My losses are of inestimable value." He had already drawn up a list and mainly wanted to find out from me how high a claim he should make. The list started with his personal worldly possessions—quite pitiful for a university professor. Then there followed the enumeration of objects which Fräulein Klara had lost in the fire. The main portion of the inventory consisted of a concise description of his scientific library of approximately eight thousand volumes which had all been burned up, with the exception of about three hundred especially valuable and rare pieces which he had relocated in the country shortly before the beginning of the bombings. The concluding paragraph mentioned his manuscripts and notes and his other ongoing studies. I gave him advice, without much hope, however, but according to my best knowledge, and after we had finished we drank a little glass of schnapps. But when I thought he was about to take his leave, he asked me, with an apologetic glance toward my wife, who left the room at once, to assure the privacy of our conference, and said: "Of course it was unconscionable, but I was very young, and prehistory was my dream, and there were no witnesses. It was in Hallstatt and the grave was unusually well-preserved and the skeleton and the artifacts completely undamaged. Of course you can say that it was a theft, particularly you as a lawyer, but I—please understand me—for me it was something else: the life of my life. And not even my Klara knew about it. It was a permanently locked cabinet and only when I was completely alone did I open the chest, and at its sight I rediscovered anew the Middle Ages and indeed all the Ages which had kept written records, instead of—quite simply, like this fellow . . . ." His voice gave out, the old man collapsed inwardly, as if the loss of that skeleton had been his own, then he suddenly rose, gave me his hand, begged my forgiveness and went to the door. The he turned around once more and said to me: "And Klara, good Klara, was in total despair because all the books had gone to hell." And shaking his head he walked out.

And I was also close to walking out and going from door to door to inform the people what kind of bones those had been which they had found among the ruins. Meanwhile my wife entered the room and I wanted to tell her the story, but I didn't tell her anything nor did I tell anyone else. The unconsummated experience with the Celt who had died two and a half thousand years earlier had transformed Fräulein Klara in all of our consciences into a woman, and it seemed to me that this was a higher truth than the facts I had just learned. I wanted to be alone for a little while and indulge in my thoughts, and I went to the pub across the street. And there sat Herr Pühringer and Fräulein Klara in front of a large and a small beer. When she saw me she blushed a little but she returned my greeting as unselfconsciously as is possible between members of the opposite sex. Then I knew that I would continue to keep my silence.

Later, by the way, the actual circumstances did become known, allegedly according to a notification by the dwarfish Armed Forces official; but that could no longer alter anything. Herr Pühringer especially did not permit himself to be distracted and took Klara as his wife and she, with her forty-seven years, still bore him a child. The godfather was the Professor, standing proxy for the Celt.

The Naked Truth

When he arrived at the Forest-Café her car was already there. Slightly irritated, he looked at his watch, but he was not late. He parked his car far away from hers, made doubly sure that it was locked and then walked inside. It was nine o'clock in the morning on a workday: the café was completely empty. In the "Salon," the larger of the two dining rooms, which one entered directly from the road, there were piled two dozen clean tablecloths on one of the fragile little tables made of tin and plastic. All the windows stood wide open, and above the pale gray and blue tiled floor curled the black extension cord of a vacuum cleaner. In the wood-paneled "Stüberl," on the other hand, whose door stood half open, not even the curtains had been pulled aside, and above the solid wooden tables still hung the rest of the cigarette smoke and the darkness of the previous night. Nonetheless he quickly glanced inside, but no one was there. Then he stepped outside onto the terrace. He felt especially like whistling to himself because he was in a very good mood.

She sat with her back to the house next to the railing, just above the little stream which made its way, gently murmuring, through the forest ground covered with brown needles; it was not a deep little stream, but in the shadow of the spruces and firs the water appeared thick and heavy so that one could not see the bottom. He bent over her hair, but at that moment she turned her head and only gave him her hand, and he thought that no one would have seen. He kissed her hand and pulled up a chair in the crunchy gravel and sat down; and then he spoke of his joyful surprise that she had time for him today. But he could not finish because the waitress came to take their order. And after they were alone again and he wanted to finish his interrupted sentence, she said, stiffly and staring ahead into the forest, with a voice as dry as wood: "Splendid! You behaved splendidly last night!" He did not see her lips moving at all, only that they were suddenly turning almost white. But not a single sound had been lost: the sentence stood between them as invisible and as tangible as a wall of glass. From the little stream and from the trees he sensed a cool humidity which seemed to freeze momentarily on the railing and on the table top, and from the open kitchen window he heard a few polka rhythms, as odd as thunder in the winter. And with great effort he tried to recall what had happened yesterday. Around five he had gone to Willy Tschapek, who not only enjoyed eating and drinking in the narrow, dusky little back room of his delicatessen shop but also liked the company of some of his regular paying patrons. These were primarily academics and businessmen, also actors and writers, almost exclusively men, most of them in their forties and fifties. One drank Danish beer and Austrian Burgundy and occasionally also champagne; one ate meat pies and river-trout and caviar with salty crackers and sometimes merely a sausage roll brought from a nearby store, and one of the guests paid for the bottle of wine and another paid for the can of trout and yet another for the champagne and the fourth one nothing at all. No one was petty. Willy, too, from time to time, of his own accord, placed a bottle on the table. And there was talk of a recently published book or of the difficulty of becoming a member of the "Geographic Society," and an agricultural engineer spoke of the draining of marshy land, and a lawyer, who was well-known as a magician, occasionally performed one of his little tricks and then he would kiss the hand of the lady who had drawn or cut the card with a grin that begged her pardon. And some came there to discuss business matters: Frau Exler, for example, the owner of Exler-Records was there almost every afternoon. Yesterday she had also been there with two television-people whom he did not know, and opposite these two sat a young man and a young girl who were entirely preoccupied with each other: they looked alternately into their glasses and into each other's eyes. Then the magician arrived, drank a beer, ate a roll and a piece of sausage taken from his briefcase and then read the newspaper which someone had left behind. And then Doctor Fritsch arrived. With her. They greeted each other; he casually kissed her hand which she held out to him and they talked about trivial things in which they had become quite practiced. He remembered exactly: She had asked him whether he'd been to Salzburg this summer, and then they had talked about the hotels and restaurants in Salzburg and that Salzburg was no longer worth the trouble since "Est est est" no longer existed, where the fish tasted as if they had just been pulled out of the water and where the Barolo wine had cost six schillings, the best Barolo in the world only six schillings, and similar things. He remembered exactly: nothing could possibly have happened. And then the opera singer Silbermann had arrived; he had a premiere that evening and drank a few little glasses of vodka. The magician read aloud from the newspaper about some sex crime and dissected the opposing expert opinions of the legal medical officers. And Silbermann gave a report to Frau Exler of his Russian tour. All others, aside from him and the magician who was buried in his newspaper, sat at the opposite end of the long table, to the left and the right of Frau Exler, next to whom the opera singer was pacing two steps back and forth. And Doctor Fritsch was leaning against the wooden beams of the stairs leading to the cellar, nibbling nuts from a can, and suddenly, no one had given him a cue, he spoke barely audibly as if to himself: "How can one explain it: that even in the most intimate union one remains alone? This eternal state of being-divided of the two platonic halves? Is it in the nature of the thing itself or is it our fault, our failure?"

He did not easily lose his composure; but for a moment he felt all his blood draining from his body. Did he know? Did he suspect? Was he testing him with this question? Was he setting a trap? His confusion, which he tried at first to rinse away with a sip of beer and then to hide with the smoke of a cigarette, increased all the more, however, since the Doctor's problematic inquiry had been totally alien to him. With a sincere heart he should have replied: "No, I am very happy and certainly not alone." He forced himself to look into Doctor Fritsch's face, who created the impression that he was a great deal more interested in his nuts than in any response from him, and he almost overcame his fear—

until suddenly he had the suspicion that the Doctor had brought her along in order to pose this question in her presence and thereby set a trap. He didn't have the slightest proof of that, but he needed something to get the upper hand, and the realization that he saw through him was just what he wanted. And he said, while trying to imitate the Doctor's bored expression, "Most likely we all feel the same, it's most likely in the nature of the thing itself." And he added with intentional aloofness: "What we call love is an attempt with inept means." He was very proud of this sentence and he was convinced that he did not betray himself. The Doctor chewed on his nuts and said: "So, you too believe there is no such thing as a complete union between man and woman, an indivisible harmony between them?" And he answered: "Yes, that's what I believe too." In the meantime the two television-people had left and Silbermann had finished his story and people were regrouping around the table littered with glasses and bottles and Willy opened a can of shrimp for one of his guests. Then he had drunk the rest of his beer and left, and on the following morning at eight she had called and asked him to meet her at nine in the café, and now they were sitting here, the wall of glass separating them, and once again he felt all his blood draining from his body; however this time, this second time, he knew of no salvation since he had betrayed himself after all. His brain was an anthill but he could not figure out what he had done wrong: when and where. He kept on stirring the sugar in his coffee, which the waitress had set down before him, and from time to time he thought of the twelve full years that he was younger than she. He felt he had to say something now and he stammered into his coffee: "I had to change course . . . I wasn't at all prepared for it . . . How could I guess that he suspected . . ." He stopped stirring but did not drink; he twisted the cup in his cold hands and asked himself what was still left for him to do, now. And he looked at her and he saw her sitting there stiffly and trembling in this stiffness as if with an unbearable tension of her entire body. Gently he placed his hand on her bare arm.

The coffee spilled over: she withdrew from him with such a violent movement. And it was not until now that she spoke, very softly, as if from very far away, from deepest exhaustion: "How could you betray me! How could you betray in such a cowardly way all that we had! How could you!" He tried to explain to her that he simply had done everything that seemed appropriate to avoid betrayal. He said: "I wasn't even quite certain whether he suspected or not. I thought: perhaps it's a trap and I tried not to fall into the trap. Forgive me, please forgive me if I did it wrong!" And then he added: "Of course I take full responsibility for everything." She let him finish, but evidently she hadn't even listened to him. And when she began to speak again her voice was still very soft and enveloped with an almost palpable melancholy, yet hard and firm: like iron in cotton wool. She said: "'An attempt with inept means'! There you have it. For me, of course, it was something else. There you have it." And now he finally understood. But she had already risen and left without a word of greeting, with crunching steps across the gravel of the terrace, and this crunching he felt in his very heart and also much later: in every thought of her, in every memory (as if clawing with fingernails) of her, in the dry chafing of his unstilled longing for her; and always in the realization that in the short conversation with her unsuspecting husband he had lied, to be sure, but yet, and actually for that reason, had spoken the truth.

A Nice Victory

"Will you tell him about it?" he asked afterwards. They were still sitting in front of their refilled glasses of whiskey in his *garçonnière* where, quite by chance, they had been left alone for a few hours. After they had been very perceptibly alone, he had put out his cigarette which he had just lit and said: "We should take a walk or go to a café. Otherwise I can't bear it not to embrace you." She had only laughed in his face and said: "Then why don't you do it!" That's how simple it had been, what he had intended for such a long time. And now he was proud of the fact that again, yes, once again, he had been confirmed in his opinions on marriage, in his views of fidelity and happiness. And he asked her: "Will you tell him about it?" For after all: they had been friends since their school days.

She arched her back, leaned back a little, closed her eyes, stretched out her arms and closed and opened her little fists several times. "Yes: I think so."

"And what will he say?"

She nestled her little head between her bare arms, which were sticking out white from her red, sleeveless blouse; she smiled a little, as if under her skin; and after a pause of listening she said: "He'll ask me if it was nice."

He thought about how unspeakably nice it had been, and then he heard her say: "My husband" and he noticed at once that she now said "my husband," whereas it had always been: "André"—: he heard her say: "My husband is the most wonderful man in the world. There's absolutely nothing about me that he doesn't love, absolutely nothing. Therefore he'll ask me if it was nice. Yes, really: my husband is the most wonderful man in the world."

He raised his glass a bit too hurriedly and several drops ran down his chin and he wiped them away with the back of his hand. She handed him a napkin and gave him a very bright and then a very sad look; for suddenly he struck her as someone who had terribly overexerted himself.

"Wie einst, Lili Marlen"

At the exit of the newsreel movie theater, shoved and pushed from behind, he happened to step on the ankle of the woman in front of him. Her knees gave way, he supported her for a moment by sliding his hand under her elbow, and said: "Please forgive me, surely I didn't hurt you seriously?" She turned her head and cried, her mouth opened only for a moment, "No, not at all!" Then she took a few steps to test her injured ankle, and her lower lip disappeared entirely between her teeth. He thought of her ankle and looked into her face and said: "You should sit down for a while to let your foot recover. May I ask you to have an espresso with me? The Café Central is just across the street. It'll be good for you to sit down for a while." She was his age and she was almost his height, and as she then walked the two hundred steps to the café, leaning on his arm, she seemed very familiar to him, yet he knew not quite what to say. He merely asked: "Is this better?" and "Don't you want to rest?" and "Is it still hurting?" Meanwhile they had entered the café and sat down by a large window in the front. Beyond the intersection the signboard of the newsreel theater was blinking and they looked over and spoke of the films which they had just seen. But the cartoon had not been all that amusing and the cultural documentary not all that interesting and the newsreel they had already seen at other movie houses. He asked her: "Do you often go to the movies?"

"Actually, yes. What else is one to do?" And after a pause: "I am divorced."

"Yes," he said. And then: "I'm not yet."

It took a long time for the waitress to come. She was wearing, like all the others, a light green little apron over her black dress, and in her hair a kind of tiara made of green beads. He ordered two large espressos and some sweets, and after the waitress had left she said: "There used to be only waiters here."

He said: "Yes. Service used to be much faster."

She asked: "Do you often come here?"

He said: "I haven't been here for a long time. I barely recognized the place. It is—it is so gaudy now and it used to be so severe. And so serene," he added; for not very far from them a jukebox started up with "Sugar Baby," and at the neighboring table someone was humming along but was incapable of keeping up with the beat.

"There used to be red plush sofas here," she said, "instead of the green synthetic little chairs. Do you remember?"

"Oh yes."

"And not these fire screens made of green glass and not the oleanders in the middle of the room."

"Definitely not."

"Of course then there was no bar with all that chrome either."

"Of course not."

"And certainly not the jukebox. A jazz orchestra had played instead; over there on the left used to be the podium, do you remember?"

"Yes, to be sure, I remember. I used to come here occasionally."

"But now all that has been changed for some time."

"Since when?"

"Three years perhaps, or four, I'm virtually never here. I don't like espresso bars."

"Yes, it's true: it has become a huge espresso bar."

After a pause she said: "Right after the war it was still nice here."

He said: "The last time I was here was during the war. I never came after the war."

"Yes, well." He had ordered brandies. She placed her hands around the tall, balloon-shaped glass, whirled it gently, and sniffed it from time to time, and then she asked him: "You were a soldier?"

He replied: "Yes."

"Also at the front?"

"Not for long. Not at the beginning and not until the end. I didn't enlist until '42, in the spring, and then in the fall I ended up in Russia, directly in Stalingrad, and then—well, you can imagine."

She spoke very softly: "Was it bad? I mean: imprisonment?"

He laughed a little: "As you can see: I survived it." And then without laughing: "It simply lasted a terribly long time. I was among the last to return home." The jukebox was howling "Rock Around the Clock," he pulled out his cigarette case and said: "A brandy calls for a cigarette." She declined. He took out a cigarette for himself and lit it. She, meanwhile, reached for the cigarette case. It was made of silver and displayed delicately engraved Arabic ornaments on both sides. "How pretty! Oh, let me see!" But she looked with her fingers instead of with her eyes: in the roughness of the engraving her fingers felt the charm of its beauty. She sat facing him. He laid down his cigarette, leaned forward, close to her face, which was turned sideways, and asked, almost in a whisper: "Why, why didn't you say anything?"

Her fingers held still, her face remained turned sideways, and she asked, just as softly, however into the expanse of the room: "You mean you really didn't recognize me?"

He replied: "No. Not until now."

She said: "I recognized you immediately. I knew you right away from your voice."

He said: "No, it's true. Not until now. With the silver case in your hand. You always liked to hold it."

"Yes."

"And as you were holding it just now, it suddenly was as it used to be."

"Yes."

"When the red plush sofas were here . . . ."

"Yes."

"And the music over there on the left . . . ."

"Yes."

"And no glittering bar . . . ."

"Yes."

"And no jukebox . . . ."

"Yes."

"And everything."

They were silent for a while and then he asked her: "Does your ankle still hurt?"

She shook her head violently: "No, not at all." Then they were silent again, but their hands were joined. And then all at once she said: "Our song. That was our song." He looked at her uncomprehendingly, and she said: "You were humming it to yourself."

He said: "Really? I wasn't even aware of it. I don't even remember the words any more."

"And you used to dictate them to me," she said. "By heart. And I wrote them into my little notebook—"

"In shorthand," he interrupted her.

"Yes, in shorthand. I still remember the bench on which we were sitting, down by the quay—"

"Although it was very foggy." Suddenly he rose and fished for a schilling in his pocket. "If we're lucky—old things are now becoming fashionable again." He walked to the jukebox, selected a record after some searching, and returned to the table.

"It was a Sunday afternoon," she said. "You were not on duty, we were here in the Central and it was here that we heard it together on the musical request program—"

"Yes, I remember." But now a different voice was singing it, a very young, very innocent, very optimistic voice, as if from a retort, totally without the sweet timbre of the knowledge of transitoriness. Therefore he quickly paid and they left. Behind them the jukebox started to roar again, and outside clung a spring evening of almost sticky warmth. In front of them, high on a façade, with flickering glowing letters, the latest news was rolling off, and next to them, in the road, the glittering chain of cars with already turned-on lights. All this they did not notice yet. They walked past a movie theater and she said: "It was here that we saw the film *Ochsenkrieg*."

"Yes. And at another time a film with Tilden, I can't recall the title, but she arrived in the country in a black tailcoat and top hat, she was probably working at a cabaret, and something happened on the farm at the dunghill, but can you believe it—I don't recall the title!"

She didn't remember the title either and said: "We also saw *Ohm Krüger* together."

"At the Metropolis."

"Yes, right: at the Metropolis. And then afterwards, outside, we were enraged and furious at the English. I remember that exactly. But the nicest part of the film was the ballet."

"It was almost warlike, a dance of precision, like a parade. At least thirty girls." And after a pause he continued: "The movies were the only thing we had then." They walked along luxurious store windows, whose lighting virtually catapulted the displayed wares out onto the street, and they walked past merrily babbling, gesticulating people, past cheerful Saturday evening faces. "Even smokers had a rough time. I had never been a heavy smoker, but without your cigarette card I never would have managed."

She said: "It wasn't much. Three cigarettes per day, I believe." He thought it had been more than that, but she said: "Only three, at the most four. Men received twice as many. But we women got only three or four."

He said: "You only received three or four because we had gotten advance ration. The tobacconist didn't even accept the November stamps, and only the waiter in the Kerzenstüberl took them, and the December stamps as well, but for those he gave us one less: he couldn't risk it because everything was being rationed even more, and cigarettes certainly had to be. Therefore he only gave us four cigarettes instead of five. But four were still better than none."

"Amazing—all the things you remember," she said close to his ear.

"And you I didn't even recognize!"

They walked on in silence for a while. "I don't know: have I changed a great deal?" she then asked.

"You've become more slender."

"And you are no longer so terribly skinny as you used to be."

"Was I really so skinny?"

"Yes, you were." She stopped, opened her purse, searched for a photo. He exclaimed: "You still have it?" and she quickly lowered it into the depth of her bag. "I lost yours in Russia. They took everything away from me, letters and photos too."

"This was it, wasn't it?" she had pulled another photo from her bag and handed it to him. They were standing in front of the entrance of a hotel restaurant, and next to the entrance, in a kind of recess, hung a menu with at least a hundred dishes, and the recess was brightly illuminated. And with the photo in his hand he stepped close to the recess and then said: "Yes. The Russians took it away from me." He returned the picture to her and she held it briefly in her hand, indecisively, like something which one either intends to discard or to keep, and only then did she put it back into her bag. Then he added: "Therefore you recognized me and I didn't recognize you."

She spoke from the depth of her throat: "No, that's not the reason at all." Then they walked on and left the annoying brightness of the main street for the narrower sidestreets by the Cathedral. But here too it was bright everywhere and noisy and full of activity. In one of these sidestreets she suddenly stopped and said: "My God, do you remember?"

He asked: "Remember what?"

"One time we were walking here, in the evening, just like now, and a truck was parked here, and because it was so dark you ran into it with your face, into the backside, directly with your nose—"

"Yes, you're right! I'd never thought about it again. But at that time it was awful: I was terrified as never before in all my life. I felt as if sparks were beaten from my brain. And for three days my nose felt like a cucumber."

They walked on, and after a while she said: "But since everything was dark down here, we could see the moon and the stars up there much better than today."

"Yes, that's true. Yes, today everything is very different." And then: "Probably the reason I didn't recognize you is because everything is so different everywhere."

She said: "The false brightness," and leaned more heavily into his arm. In the meantime they were walking, as if by chance, in any case without a plan, on the road behind the theater leading steeply up to the castle barracks. Chestnut trees were growing here and linden trees, and behind the fences of the yards lilac and elderberry bushes were crowded together. And several June bugs were droning and buzzing around the street lanterns which poured their light like water down upon the asphalt. He said: "What a wonderful spring evening!"

"Yes. It was autumn then. Strange."

"Why? Why strange?"

"I don't know. It just seems strange to me. I don't know why." And now they stopped in front of the barracks, in front of the large gate in whose wide arch a small group of people were gathered talking loudly in a foreign tongue: a section of the castle barracks was now turned into a refugee camp. And in another section were housed offices of the Provincial government. And in the basement there was an elegant restaurant. An illuminated banner stretched across the arch of the gate, and people were coming and going, past the group of refugees who, bathed in the neon light of the banner, stood beneath the arch and gossiped. The women in airy blouses and without stockings, the men with rolled-up shirt sleeves and jackets over one shoulder, and hats pushed back on their heads, all of them smoking. And in the courtyard and outside cars were parked, and whenever a car stopped, an older man, half admiral and half parrot, trotted over to the car, flung the door open, and after some money had been pressed into his hand, he bowed and lifted his gold-braided cap. And after the people had turned away, he quickly counted the money and put it into his purse, and afterward he strolled among the cars as if worried that one of them could be stolen from him. Here they stood, as they often had in the past. But now neither knew what they were supposed to do here. They stood now like two people who first had to consider whether they had sufficient money in their pocket to be able to enter the elegant restaurant. Thus they stood here next to each other and had to endure the suspiciously examining gaze of the parking lot attendant. And suddenly they both turned and very quickly walked down: There was no longer any point in their being here. Not a word had been spoken up there: once more, for a very brief moment, they were of one mind again, totally of one mind. Not until they had walked down did they begin to speak. He asked: "How's your foot?" and she said: "Well, I can still feel it a little." And as they passed the hotel restaurant with the endlessly long menu, he asked her whether she had had any dinner yet? And when she said no, they entered the restaurant and ate dinner and spoke about this and that: like two relatives who meet once in a blue moon. And after they had eaten, he took her home. She was limping again while walking and therefore he called a taxi. Then they stood in the door and he said: "Nice to have seen you again."

She said: "Yes, it was nice."

"And your foot? Is your foot still hurting?"

"It still hurts a little, but only a little. Tomorrow everything will be fine."

"That's good. I really was afraid I could have hurt you seriously." He kissed her hand and then realized that it was actually inappropriate out in the open. And finally he was annoyed that he had not had the taxi wait.

A Misunderstanding

Women can hardly imagine the kind of dirty talk going on among men. The jokes they tell—and aside from such jokes nothing else is ever talked about for hours and hours—these jokes are unspeakably primitive and therefore unspeakably filthy. Yet nonetheless: they are jokes. For it seems to be that men are embarrassed to speak directly of the one and only topic of interest, and for that reason they choose the playful camouflage. Women, on the other hand, once they have arrived at this subject matter—and men are not even aware of this for the most part—women speak of it like professors of medicine: with sober, blunt terminology, not in the least circumscribed. They have little patience for playfulness; their main concern is always the thing itself. Whoever wants to understand the difference between men and women need only compare the faltering graffiti, as it were, in a public men's toilet with that in the women's toilet.

But no matter: The young man had just graduated from business school and assumed his first position in the office of a large, internationally well-known shipping company. He had been with the firm for only a short time when the entire staff went on an outing to the Wachau on a specially reserved Danube steamer. The carousing had commenced on the ship already—they did not wait for the terraced hills of vineyards with their crumbling ruins extending into the forests—so that most of the excursionists no longer had an appreciative eye for the beauties of the landscape, for the historic monuments and the sights they were shown. On the trip back, in the evening dusk, they drank even more.

Many more men than women were employed by the firm and therefore the young man spent the day exclusively in the company of men, especially since the few women drew closer and closer together the more the men got drunk: they sat in small circles upstairs on deck and their wide hips facing outward formed a closed defensive front like those of barricades of wagons. There were also several girls on board, three or four, who evidently intended to make somebody's acquaintance. The young man, however, showed no interest in them since he compared them immediately with Elfi. Elfi was the only child of a widowed railway worker and she had graduated in the spring from the *Gymnasium*; her mouth always looked as if she were whistling a little song and her body, constantly vibrating, as if whipped by inaudible music; he had met her in a dancing class and they had been going together for well over a quarter of a year.

These men, with whom he had been all day, spoke, especially on the trip home, of nothing but filth. The young man was not prudish and he knew all the words; but he had never considered them important or even taken pleasure in them: he had simply heard them and then immediately forgotten them. But, here, on the steamer, from which he could not escape, here it was different: here he was sitting in the middle of a cesspool, confused and baffled, incapable of wallowing along and incapable of getting out, and all he felt was the physical sensation that all these obscenities were clinging to him, clogging his pores with a sticky slime, robbing him of his breath and binding his joints with a hardening paste. Finally, on the trip back, downstairs in the dining room, where the specially hired band was no longer playing *Heurigenlieder* but the latest hits, and a few solitary couples were dancing clumsily, finally under some credible pretext he left the heated group and climbed up on deck, yet there too he immediately ran into a group of men who were amusing themselves in the same manner as those from whom he had just escaped. They talked to him insistently and he wanted to scream, but since he was a newcomer, not just in the firm but also in the professional world, he realized that he would have to spend the rest of his life sitting in the office next to all these people and therefore he did not scream; but for a moment he tried to imagine the women to whom these men were telephoning from the office—about shopping, about the children, about the Sunday outing: nothing but model husbands and fathers, who were now wallowing together in mire and mud. He fled down into the gangway from which the engine room can be seen: the metal, coated with oil, shining dully, rubbing itself smooth with constant motion, was so clean that he felt like touching it. Meanwhile someone stood at his side again, leaned against his shoulder, someone who was inspired by the pounding of the steam pistons, to express some thoughts which he did not wish to keep to himself. In the little bar at the staircase leading to the deck he was detained by another and invited to a beer and was told a joke and already he had the impression that he had become their preferred garbage dumping place: "Have you heard this one yet?" and "I could tell you stuff, incredible stuff, for example . . . ." and "I'm not the youngest, granted, but let me tell you . . . ." and again and again: "Have you heard this one yet?" and "Let me tell you one more!" Paternally strict and conspiratorially soft and triumphantly lurid and wearily professing—thus they talked to him. Once again he was sitting at one of the tables in the hall and barely aware of the person talking, although he had met quite a few of these people: week after week he was sent to different departments so that he'd become acquainted with the entire operation, and therefore he knew many people, but now on the boat, he did not know who it was who was talking to him insistently. He only saw, as if cut out from a canvas and hung too closely before his eye, a fleshy thumb beneath the taut suspenders, a greasy strand of black hair dangling onto a pale forehead, a gaping shirt zipper revealing half the chest, and a winking mouth, as if it were an eye, and again and again this drawing together of heads, as if to form a bud, and then their screaming outbursts, when their upper bodies fell with a crash into the backs of benches or chairs. All this he saw with the precision of detachment. And just as precisely he heard, distinguished from the mushy noise of the music and the human voices in the hall, what was being said. And from these words there emerged, although he did not wish it, colorful images which at first faded very quickly and later on only reluctantly, and with these images mingled more and more often the image of Elfi, completely without his intention: she pushed herself into these already impetuous vivid images and finally, in spite of all his resistance, there was only one single image in which Elfi was moving as if she had been born into it. Violently, as if with a physical exertion of his brain, he pushed before this image an image of Elfi as he himself painted it: thinking of her purity he protected himself from all the filth assaulting his ears. Late in the evening, half an hour after his return on the excursion steamer, they were to meet. He was longing for this rendezvous, yet at the same time he was asking himself whether he, pumped up with so much smut, should dare to approach her. Then again he transformed her into his guardian angel who would lead him safely out of this hellish company, if only he himself were willing to keep himself pure. These were his thoughts, and yet he listened all the more. And then, when they were on land again and all had bidden each other farewell with the typical ramblings of the drunk, and when the young man, a little late, arrived at the designated meeting place in the almost deserted Stadtpark: then he did with Elfi what he had never done with her before.

Then, after they emerged from the bushes, he did not think of her, but rather of the men with whom he had spent the whole day and he was ashamed of what he had done to Elfi; in cold despair he wished he could somehow undo it. She, however, as soon as they were out of earshot of other couples and nocturnal strollers, said: "I've been waiting all these months for you to love me as you loved me today. Loved me, wonderfully loved me!" She pressed close to him and repeated again and again: "Loved me, wonderfully loved me!" And she added: "And I almost believed that you didn't love me." And again: "Loved me, wonderfully loved me!"

After the seemingly unbearably long evening at her front door, he hurried to the brothel which he had visited several times before he had met Elfi. And not until then and there could he stop feeling ashamed. On the contrary: he suddenly had to laugh loudly.

A Friend of the Family

1

Walter Patzak was an obliging young man. He had not only saved the lady's shoe, whose stiletto heel had been caught in the escalator, but he also called a taxi for her since the broken heel now impeded her walking. He also could not forego accompanying her in the taxi up to her front door. He was not, to be sure, a bold young man; he simply had to go in the same direction, too. She, visibly touched by so much good will, asked him upstairs and offered him a cup of tea. They sat at a little ebony table before an open game of cards. "Here I sit and play solitaire," she told him, rearranging a few cards. "Red queen on the black king, black knave on the red queen . . . ." Although he had not found an appropriate reply he was, nonetheless, offered an invitation: for Saturday evening at eight o'clock. "You must tell me a lot about your job. It must be terribly interesting to be a reporter!" He did not, as it turned out, have to tell all that much. They did not sit at the game table but rather on the couch. And they did not merely sit. He was, after all, a thoroughly obliging young man.

On the following Saturday they also met again on the couch, and then on a Tuesday morning. And then on a Sunday at noon, and then again and again. They had become quite accustomed to these meetings.

And had become correspondingly careless.

So that one day the Department Head Remigius Chloupka discovered, quite by chance, some clues. And then, not quite by chance anymore but rather in the vein of a semi-criminalistic search, in his wife's night stand, a photo. With a dedication.

Two souls, alas, dwelled in his breast; one of these remained quite untouched by the discovery, thereby enraging the other all the more. This latter soul spoke to him: "My poor Remigius, look, what else can you do but be frightfully furious?" And, therefore, he was frightfully furious. Had his wife been present, she would have witnessed her otherwise always rosy smiling husband as pale and berserk. She, however, was sitting in a café and leafing through magazines. Thus, it was only her innocent couch that heard her husband's insults and accusations. For ten entire minutes. Then the solitary accuser grew tired of railing against a mere piece of furniture and in the ensuing silence he also heard the other soul: "What do you wish, Department Head, sir? Do you want a divorce? Do you want a trial on account of a marriage disturbance? Or do you perhaps even want a duel? In short, do you wish a scandal?"

Of course, he did not want that. He still believed, however, that he owed it to his other soul to be frightfully furious. And, therefore, he tore his hair and ripped his clothes, the latter only symbolically, by opening his shirt collar, whereby he seized upon the idea of ripping up the photo. It was a cheap passport photo and showed the head of a young man with a broad face, with hair falling on his forehead like Marlon Brando as Mark Antony, with large questioning eyes and a likewise questioning open mouth. Everything very earnest, almost stupid. But actually, a nice young man on whom one could rely. In spite of the inscription on the back: "For Regine, my secret queen, from Walter, March 24."

For at least three months they've been carrying on, Remigius Chloupka was thinking, and Department Head Chloupka continued to think that these three months had been particularly pleasant for him. Totally without any altercation with her and she had expressed amazingly few desires and had not reproached him and not over-exerted him as had been the case from time to time in the past. Yes, what is more, during these three months she had been as considerate, as good-natured, as understanding as never before, and as affectionate and gentle as she hadn't been in a long time. In short, fortune had entered his home, and the fact that it had not actually entered but had stealthily crept in, did not lessen his will to hold on to it now. Therefore, he returned the photo to its secret place in the night stand, smiled encouragingly at himself in the mirror, and enthusiastically clapped his hands. And he left his apartment to instruct a detective agency with the following two assignments: to discover the name, profession, address and circumstances of the young man, and to make complete notations of continued proceedings. The Department Head, Remigius Chloupka, was understandably a skeptic as far as his wife, twenty years his junior, was concerned.

2

Said young man had studied journalism for five and a half semesters and had been working for barely a year at the *Evening Post*. In the local section, and at the lowest level. He was constantly underway, but the events to which he was sent—to harmless traffic accidents and apartment fires and domestic fights and similar events which appeared at best as announcements in the smallest print, never as reports—these events were much too lacking in sensationalism to merit being published. He worked virtually only for the wastepaper basket. Yet once he had dreamed of headline articles.

Then one simply has to dream of other things. One dreams, for example, of two legs standing before one on the escalator. In the editor's office there was a certain Mitzi with whom he had been involved for six or seven weeks, with whom he associated the smell of reheated cabbage. These legs here, however . . . and suddenly it had happened. And one was sitting with her on the couch. And not just sitting. One was, after all, yes, what was it that one was? One was a real devil of a fellow, otherwise how could one ever have escaped from Mitzi and landed here?

Here, in this apartment with its muted light and heavy, thick curtains, where one was offered an aperitif before the meal and where one did not eat cabbage and dumplings but fondue or sautéed brain. Here, where a smell never overwhelmed a room but faintly lingered beside two or three other scents just as delicate. Here, where names were mentioned and incidents discussed which otherwise one only encounters in newspapers (and naturally not in the local section). Where words fell as softly as shadows, and even the telephone, instead of ringing shrilly, merely hummed. Here, in real life. An undressed woman (Walter Patzak confirmed this to his amazement and satisfaction) is basically no different from any other undressed woman; it is only the couch on which she is lying and the scent enveloping her that makes the difference. Not the woman herself, but her milieu transforms the man, whom she receives, into a better person, Walter Patzak was thinking. And he felt very much a better person and now, more than ever, he suffered from all the harmless traffic accidents, apartment fires, and domestic fights that never made it into the newspapers.

Therefore, he had immediately made up his mind to apply for the position which had been offered to him in writing: "Upon a recommendation from members of the press," it stated literally in the official-looking letter. He did not waste much time wondering who his unknown patron could be. At the appointed hour, with correctly knotted tie and shined shoes, he stood in the dim hallway of the Ministry of Commerce in front of door number 118, knocked vigorously, though not brutally, and at the same moment read the name plate: Department Head Dr. R. Chloupka/Reception. A soprano voice from within called: "Come in!"

Therefore, enter! Despite the most ardent desire to exit!

"I have come—I merely wanted to inquire—"

"Mr. Patzak?"

He thought, No, no mention of my name. I have simply mistaken the door! And he nodded.

"Please, be so kind and take a seat. Our Department Head will be pleased . . . ."

He was not quite seated when a rosy smile, from behind the noiselessly opened, cushioned door, flowed into the secretary's office and before he could have jumped up he was already enveloped by a cushioned handshake which virtually transported him into the Department Head's office. And twenty minutes later he was, even though at first only on trial, editor of the monthly magazine *World and Homeland*, the official organ of the Foreign Tourist Agency. "The issues are too colorless, too pale," the Department Head had said to him. "And you, Mr. Patzak, seem to us to be the right man to suffuse it with new life: modern ideas, an optimistic spirit."

3

The Department Head had clearly convinced himself that his wife's relationship with the young man would not last if it were constantly exposed to endangerments and burdens dealing with total secrecy. And, furthermore, that he would have to exert control over the young man financially, and therefore morally, in order to be able to restrain or goad him on, according to his wishes, yes, even more: in order always to be able to give direction to this entire game of chance.

Severe people will perhaps disapprove of the Department Head's behavior; however, he acted in the spirit of neighborly Christian love. What, after all, did he offer his pretty young wife? During the day he sat in the Ministry; granted, others spent forty-five hours per week in front of a lathe. On free afternoons and in the evenings, there were often meetings in the Foreign Tourist Office, at the Institute for Space Research, at the Board for Environmental Protection, at the Vienna Woods Society, at the Committee for Urban Beautification, at the Society for Foreign Friends. Or he had to attend a dinner with the Minister, or cocktails for the Press, or a conference for editors. Or he had to take foreign visitors to the Capuchin Catacombs and to the wine gardens in Grinzing and afterwards, to top it all, to the Eden Bar. And on weekends he had to travel more extensively, the more responsibilities and offices he accumulated: to Lugano for a conference with Czech colleagues, to Linz for the opening of the freeway-access, to Baden-Baden to give a lecture on spas in the East-Alpine region, to Warsaw for the dedication of the official Austrian Travel Bureau, to Munich for a roundtable discussion on TV concerning integration in tourism, to Kitzbühel regarding the opening of a new gondola. (He certainly did not have any time left for his electric train set.) No, his wife did not, after all, derive much pleasure from his company. And since their son was in Liebenau at boarding school, she had to feel even more lonely and neglected. Therefore, he continued to reason, her extravagant wishes: every few weeks a new hat, which, as soon as it was purchased, no longer pleased her. And the stereo set with the innumerable Karajan recordings. And instead of the Fiat, a Sunbeam (to which, however, he had not yet given his approval). No, she did not derive much pleasure from his company, all the more since he felt, in his deepest soul, yet with fullest consciousness, that the institution of marriage was not much different from a home-bordello, so to speak. To be sure it was not cheaper, but more comfortable, and without fear of syphilis.

And, he continued to think he could enjoy even greater comfort if he could delegate everything too strenuous, too boring or too expensive to this nice young man: for example, the buying of hats or Karajan recordings. He, the Department Head, was no longer among the youngest, and moreover, rather moderate. The nice young man had been terribly confused and had stammered all sorts of nonsense. Yet, he, the Department Head, had rather liked him. He liked the young man—who was sitting between two chairs or more precisely between the couch and the editor's chair—in spite of the perspiration that had crept above his too tight collar, even though the Department Head had conducted himself with immense tact: never stared at him directly, only flattered him with his joviality. Yes, he had rather liked the young man. Only one thing annoyed him: the fact that he had offered him 3,000 schillings; 2,500, he felt, would have sufficed since it was a matter of holding him on a short leash. On the other hand, he recalled: the hats! And: it's not my money anyway. If he buys her a hat every month, the Sunbeam will gradually pay for itself. And he placed a telephone call to the General Manager's Office.

4

Walter Patzak staggered through the dusky hall and down the staircase into the street. He tore his tie and also inadvertently his collar-stud from his neck. And he took a deep breath. And thought. So that is the brutal fellow responsible for driving his wife into an adulterous relationship!

That was actually, as he established without satisfaction, a moral response. However, it was inappropriate for the just-discovered reality. For the Department Head had been absolutely charming. Yes, even more. He had shown himself to be a man whom one does not betray. At least not with a good conscience. In the realm of the couch he had often tried to imagine the husband of this woman. And always he had turned out a haggard, yellow, laconic boor and not this rosy smile and this cushioned handshake. He had pictured him as a frenzied slave driver, yet he encountered a man who was sitting at his desk like a carouser at the *Heurigen* enjoying his third *Viertel* of wine. No, Walter Patzak thought, he was not the type of man to neglect his wife. And, since he was riding a moral wave, he was ready here and now to put an end to this affair. But he did not know how to go about it. And therefore he preferred to think of the 3,000 schillings—for a part-time job. For it had been the explicit wish of the Department Head that he not yet give up his position at the *Evening Post*.

He stood for a long time in front of a car dealer's store. He stood there for so long that he began to think again of all the harmless traffic accidents (and apartment fires and domestic fights) which never made it into the newspaper. And in this connection he recalled Mitzi (and a few earlier Mitzis). As a person he was a moral being, but nevertheless he was not so readily willing to abandon conquered positions. Never again, he told himself, back to the smell of reheated cabbage!

Therefore, if things were to continue, he had to talk to her at once. And he called her and shortly thereafter visited her to tell her everything. But the couch swallowed everything that he wanted to tell her. She did not find out about it until evening, in bed, from her husband. After he had turned out the light—in order to spare her any possible embarrassment.

He said, "Yes, one more thing. I have made some breathing space for myself. Look, I simply can't handle the magazine any longer on top of all the other business in the Union and on the Board. I need some help. And someone recommended to me a young man, very promising and ambitious, a local reporter from the *Evening Post.*"

He paused briefly to give her the opportunity to inquire about the young reporter's name and to hear whether she was holding her breath. The latter she did, the former not.

Thus he continued, "His name is Watzek. Or Patzek. Or something similar. In any case, he was most warmly recommended by the *Evening Post* and I believe I can rely on him. You'll have to meet him sometime. I'd like to hear your opinion. You women very often have the better instinct." And after a second pause in which he listened whether she was breathing faster: "We old cowards always want to manage everything by ourselves. One must also give youth a chance, don't you think?" And then: "Good night, sweetheart!" And suddenly, after renewed well-measured pause, he rolled over to her and said: "And something even more important that I've almost forgotten to mention to you"—her breathing seemed to stop entirely—"I ordered the Sunbeam for you today." And he believed he could notice her effort to sob.

She sobbed, but without any effort. She sobbed simply because all these words at once had been too much for her. And she said, "Dearest I don't deserve that." He merely mumbled, because basically he was of the same opinion. And he listened to her continuing (without realizing, to be sure, how deeply annoyed she was by Walter's lack of an explanation): "No, really, I don't! I don't deserve that at all!" Heavy swallowing. "You work yourself to death in order to make me happy"—she embraced his neck with her arm—"and I? What do I do?" He was growing uneasy. "I"—very heavy swallowing—"I do things . . . ."

Everything in him said: "Stop!" And his mouth too said it, formulated differently of course. "I don't like discussions, I like something else," said his mouth and not merely his mouth.

He received the kiss, of course. Then he told her that she made him unhappy with her self-reproaches, no matter what the reasons, and that he did not wish to be unhappy, but happy instead. And he devoted himself to her in such a way that made it virtually impossible for her to continue discussing the matter.

5

After this happily mastered crisis, things went pretty smoothly for a while. Walter Patzak divided his by now relatively scarce time between the foreign tourist trade, the traffic accidents, and the couch. And he was happy. And lost weight. Whereas the Department Head Chloupka, out of sheer happiness, put on additional fat. And his wife kept asking herself why she could have been so foolish, at that time, as to want to confess her affair.

But then things almost took a tragic turn, that is, when Walter Patzak came to the Chloupkas for dinner. He was so confused that he let himself be helped out of his soaking wet raincoat by the Department Head personally. In the living room, his hand-kiss miscarried: in order to demonstrate its innocuousness, he had not approached his hostess sufficiently. In the living room, the aperitif was offered and he sat beside her on the couch. And one simply sat there. In his state of agitation, he dropped his burning cigarette which rolled beneath the couch. And he felt, not unrightly so, very odd kneeling with extended rear to retrieve the cigarette. At last they sat down to dinner. The Department Head devoured his while the other two struggled with their food. The Department Head poured the wine, again and again, but the two others were not released in the slightest from their constraint. The Department Head addressed his editor with "my dear young friend," and that was all the more inappropriate since these were the very words which his wife also said to her Walter. The young man grew fiery-red and the Department Head's wife (they were already enjoying an espresso) suddenly had to go to the kitchen to fetch some sugar, although a full sugar bowl was standing on the table. After these terribly embarrassing moments, the Department Head led his guest up to the attic to his model train set, which he had set up on a separate space of almost five hundred square feet: with train stations and tunnels and villages and a sawmill and grazing cows and a gondola. He explained everything and set a train in motion. Walter Patzak, however, was thinking. He can well afford this, this childish pastime! And in the meantime he repaired—for he was, after all, an obliging young man—with a few agile movements of the hand a defective switch signal.

This gave the Department Head an idea. But before he went about realizing it, he organized a cocktail party, two weeks after this unfortunate dinner, for people from the Foreign Tourist Agency, from the Board, from the Vienna Woods Society, and for several office colleagues. Walter Patzak, too, was invited and introduced as the new editor of *World and Homeland* as well as a friend of the family. No one was supposed to be surprised by the young man's comings and goings.

The cocktail party was, at least for Chloupka's purposes, a complete success; moreover, there was no miscarried hand kiss, no burning of cigarettes beneath the couch. To facilitate this young man's frequent comings and goings and assure his clearest conscience, the Department Head asked him in front of several witnesses to take an interest—should his spare time permit it and not be occupied in more pleasant ways—in the electric installation of his model train set. "The entire system, unfortunately, is quite corroded, and I personally, as you know, no longer have the time for it, and I don't know half as much about electrotechnics as you do, my friend. Perhaps sometime you would care to put it in order?"

Of course, he would certainly like to do that! It's just that it would take much time and he had to come at least twenty times, which was not at all surprising considering the size of the system. And thus the young man was taken in by the Chloupkas and further dinners together took place (occasionally the Department Head had to leave for a certain reception or a meeting)—and these further dinners proceeded very harmoniously. And not merely the dinners. Everyone was—for various reasons to be sure—very satisfied and completely happy, especially during those times when they succeeded in ignoring their secret fears: the Department Head's wife's fear that her husband might discover her affair; Walter Patzak's fear that he might not be able to afford the hats and records (what luck that he had not given up the *Evening Post*!) and the Department Head's fear that his wife might have the impulse again to make a confession. Therefore, from time to time, he made quite liberal speeches maintaining that especially in the most intimate matters each person was only responsible for himself and that one's personal conscience triumphed above all conventions. Until he experienced another fear: that his wife perhaps might sense that he was speaking *pro domo*.

6

She would not have been entirely wrong in this regard. For in Lugano and Munich and Bratislava and Kitzbühel, the Department Head displayed a barely hidden interest for wide bottoms and buxom breasts: usually those of chambermaids and waitresses, but also those of secretaries and streetwalkers. The main point: short and fat, for his wife was tall and slender. In short, on his trips he enjoyed his dalliances. One flirted and fondled, and sometimes more than just flirted and fondled: whatever a man requires after a day full of strenuous conferences and speeches, tours and receptions. From Walter Patzak, of course, who had to accompany him more and more frequently, he kept these nocturnal activities secret. His wife must not learn of them. It was not until after the misfortune had befallen him that he realized he should have done just the opposite: that is, kept his wife's lover informed. A Department Head, too, grows wiser only after the damage has been done.

The detective agency, which had continued to note diligently Walter Patzak's visits, reported as of late a decreasing frequency. Still, the husband was struck as if by a bolt from the blue: "Dearest, I have seen a hat—simply enchanting! Please, please!" For well over a year now he had not had to buy her a hat. She had, as she reassured him, always bought the hats herself—with saved housekeeping money. (What else should she have said!) In any case, the Department Head became panicky. He bought the hat, to be sure, but with a grinding of teeth.

On the same day he searched for and found an excuse to have a scene with his editor. "You are a treacherous person!" he screamed at him. And Walter Patzak, who thought that his affair had been uncovered, fainted. As he was swooning, however, he heard that the subject was not Regine but rather some advertisements. After he was offered the smelling salts, he could hear the Department Head apologizing and giving him a couple of days of vacation. He was loaded into a taxi and treated, free of charge, by the Chloupkas' family physician.

The senselessness of the one had brought the other one to his senses. The Department Head concluded logically that the young man's oversensitive moral attitude was in need of strengthening. Should he realize that I myself, he continued to plan, well—am not exactly prudish, then he too will have no inhibitions. It was a matter of offering the young man a clear conscience, of providing him with a moral alibi—something that proved not too difficult for the Department Head, and, since they had to travel more frequently than before, he succeeded quite quickly. And thus Walter Patzak reentered the realm of the Mitzis—in Lugano, in Munich, in Bratislava, in Kitzbühel—wherever flirting and fondling and sometimes more than just flirting and fondling was going on. And he longed less for Regine than for fondue and sautéed brain, since the Department Head frequented, whenever possible, only those public places where one ate cabbage and dumplings and drank a couple of pitchers of beer. Perhaps simply from innate inclination, more likely however out of respect for his companion, he discovered rather soon and then enjoyed wholeheartedly the joys of all that which the Department Head referred to, with an almost melancholy sigh, as the simple life: wide bottoms and buxom breasts here, cabbage and dumplings and beer there—all of which agreed visibly well with the pupil. Once, later, on the occasion of one of his less frequent visits to her apartment, when he saw the solitaire cards spread out on the little ebony table, he thought: She can well afford this, this childish pastime! And then on the couch, (and within brackets, as it were) he continued to think: We, people like us, have more serious things to do.

7

For quite some time now Walter Patzak had no longer been tormented by morals but rather only by his work: by *World and Homeland* (he was now solely responsible for editing the magazine) and by the *Evening Post*, which no longer dispatched him merely to traffic accidents, apartment fires, and domestic fights, but to tiptop press conferences with vermouth and cold buffets. His circumference as well as his self-confidence continued to increase. In the Vienna Woods Society he had advanced to secretary, and as of late, he functioned, even if panting asthmatically, as a kind of private secretary to the Department Head—because he still was an obliging young man. In his spare time he sat in the lecture halls in order to conclude his studies, almost two-thirds completed. The never totally suppressed craving for loftier matters (in spite of the simple life à la Department Head) was reawakened in the desire to be permitted to display a title. However: only very rarely did he buy hats and records. The model train set likewise, in spite of the Department Head's investigating, no longer needed any repairs. Everything worked, and it worked so irreproachably and absolutely pleasurably that Walter Patzak himself would have liked to spend a part of his time chasing the little trains over the tracks. Occasionally, that's just what he did, after he had had a second key to the attic made. The possession of this key spared him the detour via the couch. The detective, in any case, could be called off—something that eased the Department Head's financial burden to be sure, but not his worries. And then after he had been annoyed for an entire evening with Karajan recordings, he began to reflect on the uselessness of his wife's lover and that now might be the time to expedite him gently but promptly. His hitherto so cheerful life became embittered, and no doubt he would have worked himself into a terrible rage over this young man if said young man had not suddenly become ill. He had collapsed, clasping the telephone receiver in his chalk-white fist, in one of the numerous office chairs. After the initial shock, the Department Head had breathed a satisfied sigh of relief, not merely on account of the physician's diagnosis which was in no way alarming, but especially about the fact that fate had given him a tip. Obviously: things much more embarrassing in this world are being justified or explained with illness! The physician, drawn into confidential consultation, confirmed a nervous breakdown and recommended taking a cure in the mountains for several months. "Of course, the Union takes care of all expenses," the Department Head reassured the patient. There was talk of vegetative dystonia, of the thyroid, of the blood pressure, and the Department Head said to him, "My friend, you are too young to be a manager! I always say that above all one must not let things gain ground! To prevent is better than to cure! Therefore, rest for the time being, stay in bed, then go to the mountains for several months, and afterwards, my friend, you should do nothing but study until you have your doctorate. Then, of course, come back to us!" The valiantly seconding physician presupposed the damaging influences of the Viennese climate and suggested to the patient a continuation of his studies elsewhere; perhaps in Graz. "Or even better, in Zurich," the Department Head said, recalling the very rapid train connection between Graz and Vienna ever since electrification. His handshake was at least as cushioned as at that time in the Ministry, and he strode away covered from head to toe with self-praise: Well done, Remigius Chloupka!

8

But—to quote the Department Head himself—: "One must not praise the day before it's over!" After barely a week he himself stood at the edge of a nervous breakdown, and not merely on account of the Karajan recordings or the hats. His entire life had visibly fallen into disarray. To be sure, the domestic burdens were bad enough and now—since all responsibilities fell upon him—they were much worse to endure than before. However, there were also other problems. He could not meet deadlines; the magazine appeared three weeks late; urgent letters remained unanswered; calamities with the Finance Department; in Lugano or Munich or Bratislava or Kitzbühel no rooms had been reserved; the Union members received their invitation to the annual meeting the day after, and the Minister demanded a document which he was unable to locate anywhere. And the electrical system of the model train, to which he had fled in desperation, had developed a defect in its main relay which he could not repair so easily. And neither wide bottoms nor buxom breasts nor cabbage and dumplings and beer were capable of cheering up his gloomy spirits. On a Karajan recording he extinguished his cigar! Never in all the thirteen years of his marriage had he let himself be swayed to even such an approximately comparable act of brutality. On his face, instead of blooming roses, withering cabbage. At a party he heard someone whisper, "I think he's ready for retirement." And the other replied, with an almost audible, sad nodding of the head, "Prematurely worn out."

And thus the faithful physician had to approach the patient's bed and say, "Mr. Patzak, I would not have considered this possible but just by looking at you and certainly by looking at all your test results, you are completely fit." (That was, of course, true; he was only too heavy.) Ah, what rejoicing when he asserted, yes, asserted his right by resuming his obligations! Not all obligations, naturally. He was after all still in need of care, alternately swallowed Carnigen and Librium, sat in the sauna with the Department Head and took evening walks around his block. And first of all, he had to catch up with all the work which had been abandoned in the five or six orphaned offices during his hospital stay. And in between there were trips to Lugano, to Munich, to Bratislava, to Kitzbühel. And whenever he paid a visit to the Chloupkas, he was tired; and he dozed off on the couch. One time he dreamed of a cigarette which had rolled underneath it. Startled, he jumped up thinking that he had to defend himself against someone. But the Department Head was peacefully sitting in his easy chair, carefully snipping an indentation into the tip of his cigar. And from the direction of the little ebony table he heard the gentle snapping sound of cards held perhaps a little too long between thumb and index finger. An idyllic scene. Also a sort of simple life. One could continue to sleep with peace of mind.

The Department Head was not always present; or sometimes he had to rush off to a reception. Then the couch felt as if it had a memory, and its springs sounded like the humming of bees, like the harp in the Hölty poem. She did not know the poem, but since he had, after all, studied German literature, he recited it for her by heart. And for a short time things were as they had once been. But usually he only came for a visit when the Department Head, too, had a free evening. If the latter was occupied, he likewise was busy: whether behind the desk or in the sauna, whether here in the Foreign Tourist Agency or in Lugano (et cetera). Whatever things had to be done: they did them together, the Department Head and his secretary. Only where the woman and wife was concerned: that did not work out. And, therefore, nothing happened at all: neither from the husband's nor from the lover's side: both were playing upstairs with the electric train. She, however, with the indestructibility of her sex, sat once again, evening after evening, at her little table and played solitaire: red queen on the black king, black knave on the red queen . . . .

Life after Death

Spellmann, the critic, had been the first to come and say: "It has been ten years, and we thought that would be an appropriate occasion to organize a commemorative exhibit at Stockhoff & Meyer." Then Leo Lipitzky had come—he was now working for television—and had said: "You know, we'd like to put out a little book, *Voices of Friends*, with a collection of his reviews and with some new things, everyone will contribute and we'll use some graphics, Semaphor publishers will do it; I've taken care of everything." On the street she had run into Hugo Meixner the actor, and Hugo Meixner had said: "I think we should hold a graveside ceremony; the others agree with me. And I've already suggested to Sawatzki that he display the sketches of the stage settings in the foyer." And Kristan, the publisher, had paid her a visit and had said: "For the tenth anniversary we want to come out with a portfolio, either containing twelve to fifteen selected sheets, or containing the Job-Cycle, if we can get hold of all the sheets. Heinersdorff is supposed to write the introduction; he knew him better than all of us put together." And then one day all the old friends—Spellmann, Lipitzky, Meixner, Kristan and Heinersdorff—all had come together to see her in order to discuss everything and synchronize everything. And then each of them had come separately to rummage in the portfolios, to unearth old reviews, to make excerpts from letters and to look at photos. But she should have cooked and done the homework with her fourteen-year-old Harald; she had wanted to sweep the living room and she was, at the time, especially busy at the office because the draughtsman had gone into business for himself; Doctor Schinagl gave her work to take home almost daily. And now she had to rummage in the portfolios and unearth old reviews and make excerpts from letters and look at old photos; and all the while she was thinking of the unwashed dishes in the kitchen and of Peter's torn pants, and said: "Yes, this photo, if you'd like, or this one, if you prefer . . ."—for it didn't matter to her; it didn't matter at all. And she was merely amazed that so much commotion was made, now, over something that lay ten and twelve and fifteen years in the past. She would have liked to remarry, then; just for the sake of the children. But perhaps just because of the children no one had married her. He had left her two children, to be sure, but no pension and not even a savings book, and the paintings she was able to sell only right after his death, and then later on not at all; and therefore she had returned to Doctor Schinagl's office, where she had also worked before. And where they had met each other, after his accident on the motor scooter. The scar on the left temple had remained and so had his habit of fingering the indented scar with his long, white index finger, which sometimes made it seem as if he were poking around in his brain. But that had not been the worst of his habits: she had suffered much more whenever he loosened his belt, after lunch at the latest, and opened his shirt and let his belly hang out. She also could not bear it when suddenly in the middle of the day he lay down on the sofa and massaged his bared body with a little plastic brush. Truly repulsive had been his mouth odor in the evenings after he'd eaten fatty foods and afterwards drunk a schnapps, and when in bed later on he enveloped her with this stench. And when she stipulated that he brush his teeth beforehand, a fight had taken place every time. And on the whole they had fought a lot; for example, because he did not want a lamp shade in the living room, which was also his studio at the time. Usually she had been able to cope with the fighting itself but what she couldn't endure: that he would get up in the midst of an argument, walk over to the easel and patiently paint for hours on end with the most delicate little brush, stroke by stroke, with the door open, which she slammed shut again and again, and which he would open gently again and again until one day he unhinged it and leaned it against the wall. She thought of these things and she thought of the many countless mornings when he had stayed in bed while she fed the children and went shopping and began to cook, and she thought of the many countless afternoons when he sat dense and dull at the kitchen table and read half a dozen newspapers from the headline article to the very last advertisement, while she rinsed the dishes and scrubbed the floor and in between wheeled the baby carriage, and she thought of the many countless evenings when he sat with his friends in his studio and each one was more brilliant than the next, while she had to change the diapers of the little ones one more time and had to sing them to sleep, and she thought of the many countless nights when, after having worked all day, he made his solitary wanderings through the city, she lay awake and with every rattling of the children's bed she thought she heard the key turning in the lock. And she thought of everything else that had annoyed, irritated and repulsed her. And her almost sullen amazement grew larger and larger that such a commotion should take place now over something that lay ten and twelve and fifteen years back and had long since passed and should remain in the past because it had not been such that it was worth recalling. Because here was her work with her children and here was her work in the office. But since his old friends were visiting her, she rummaged in the portfolios and unearthed old reviews and made excerpts from letters and looked at photos and therefore she thought of everything yet didn't remember at all her tears that had welled up when Heinersdorff, who at that time already had been an almost famous writer, had spoken at the opening of the first exhibit of the singular courage, a courage totally incomprehensible to all others, which compels someone to undertake things in a way which previously no one else has ever done; of the courage to be alone for all eternity, so that she had silently stammered: "No, you are not alone, not now or ever!" And she did not remember how for at least two weeks afterwards she had sneaked out of the apartment very early in the mornings on some pretext and had leafed through all the newspapers downstairs at the tobacconist's and how depressed and enraged simultaneously she had been because only the *World Echo* and the *Daily Mirror* had published a review of the exhibit. She also no longer thought of the countless evenings in which she had conveyed to him her impression of a finished painting and he had then explained his intention. She no longer thought of the unnerving battle with the dragon of doubt, of this battle which only she alone was aware and no one else, because everywhere else he played the role of the satisfied radiant boor; and she no longer thought of the fireworks of his ideas which he was capable only of igniting with her and no one else; in short: she no longer thought of his struggle for self-perfection in his work, a struggle that descended into naked despair and rose to audacious heights, until finally, silently, they held each other by their hands and their mutual mental arousal subsided with their united bodies. And that no one before her was permitted to see a finished painting and that she was the only person allowed to look at his paintings in progress; that too she also no longer thought of. Forgotten was also her jubilation when he received the travel stipend to Italy; and forgotten was Italy itself. And how he had taught her there to see colors which did not even exist in the inland; and how she had watched him paint in the wide open, and how her eyes had therefore become sharper and more expansive and how her jubilation, sentenced to silence, had given rise to the highest hopes for him, had awakened in her the wildest longings for him so that she could barely wait until they reached their room and she could tear her dress from her body; and when he caressed her with his stained fingers, she felt as if he were continuing to paint on her. She also no longer thought of Herr Stockhoff's confidential words on the last day of the sale exhibit: "My dear, that was the most successful exhibit I've ever held: only six of the forty paintings remain unsold," and how she had to bite her lips in order not to say: "I, Herr Stockhoff, I have known that all along!" She no longer thought of how they selected the paintings: how he had placed her judgment above his own. And no longer of her otherwise unwonted attentiveness, with which she registered every word of the banquet speakers, when he accepted the state prize. For she had always paid homage to the work which was honored here and she felt as if it had been their mutual work which was honored here, although she never could quite bear it when, speaking of his work, he also included her: "Well, that's behind us now," or "I believe, we have reason to be pleased," or "We're doing much better things now," and similar things. All that was forgotten, just as the reception was at the French Embassy where she heard, behind her, an impudent voice asking another: "Who is the cute little thing?" and the other replied: "Why don't you talk to her and ask her!" until a third person whispered her name and then suddenly she was surrounded by the gentlemen, and one offered to bring her a glass of champagne and another wanted to light her cigarette and someone praised the incomparable paintings of her husband and yet another introduced someone to her, who lingered far too long over a hand-kiss, and another still, while raising his glass to his twinkling little eyes, insisted that not until now had he been able to explain the origin of beauty, which he had perceived in the paintings of her husband; all that was effected only by her husband's name: his name, which was also hers; because of him. Yet she no longer thought of any of this. Or yes; she did think of all this while she was rummaging in the portfolios and unearthing old reviews and making excerpts from letters and looking at pictures. She thought of it as one thinks of exaltations that one feels ashamed of five minutes later or as one thinks of childish things which have prevented one from real life. For her, now, he had been less than some small magistrate official with a warranted pension, and she considered it almost a mockery that now such a commotion was made over something that lay ten and twelve and fifteen years back, and better not to have been at all. The *Voices of Friends* was published, the portfolio with the Job-Cycle appeared, in the foyer of the *Volkstheater* hung his sketches for the stage settings, at Stockhoff & Meyer there was a commemorative exhibit, and the newspapers printed articles as long as those during his lifetime; and about a hundred people gathered around his grave. And she no longer understood all that. She would have liked to remarry at that time but no one had asked her: a thousand voices told her that now, around the grave. They spoke to her of something dead as if it were alive; but for her it had been dead for ten years and until all eternity, and then only until the next morning in the office of Doctor Schinagl: when someone knocked on the door and entered and then it wasn't he but someone else. And then she started to cry. And cried so loudly that Doctor Schinagl, a lawyer and therefore certainly not a philanthropist, sent her home. But after an hour she came back and told him: "There are certain days when women don't know what's the matter with them. I'm sorry, Doctor Schinagl; it won't happen again." And it never did happen again.

A Successful Surprise

How does one leave the morning after? One can't very well say "A thousand thanks!" or, worse, place a thousand schillings on the night stand. After all, she was a friend and not some lady from the Graben and Kärntnerstrasse. So, what does one do? Well, for example: while she is making the coffee in the next room one paints with her lipstick in capital letters "I love you" on a piece of paper and slides this piece of paper between the bedcovers and pillow of the still warm but already made bed. Anyway, that was what he did after his first visit.

Which, however, and for that very reason, was to be his last. Actually she already had a lover, and with this lover she had had a falling out, and that was the only reason she had invited the other to her room. Well, maybe. And in the evening this lover appeared, not really sure whether he was still interested or not. What he really wanted was to avoid another fight. He did want her to love him again as always and she, not so much responsive as tired (and perhaps suffering a bit from a bad conscience), told him while she was showering that he should turn down the bedcovers. And as he was turning them down, still without any real hope, he found a piece of paper on the pillow, and on this paper in garish red letters "I love you." He folded the paper quickly and slipped it into his pocket as a cherished remembrance, and the entire night he was so happy that she still loved him after all, that he, in turn, loved her now more than ever, and they became reconciled and remained together for a long long time.

Consequences of Garrulousness

He had been all over the world—unsurprisingly, since he was a correspondent for a large paper—and at times he couldn't remember whether he had eaten the Zras à la Nelson, which he was talking about, in Bucharest or in Hamburg or perhaps in Salzburg. And likewise he soon became uncertain about the bathroom in which he had seen the postcard-sized reproduction of an old Japanese picture: a woman in a foam bath, with a blue bathtowel somewhere in the front, and black lacquered boxes for her toiletries somewhere in the back. And besides, what an idea to hang a picture in the bathroom! He had never seen a picture before in any bathroom, and that was why he was now speaking of it as he and his old pals and a few others were sitting together one evening. And everyone seemed delighted that someone had had the idea to hang a little picture in a bathroom, and all were indeed delighted, except for one. And this one visited his fiancée that very night and first removed the picture from the wall and then broke off the engagement.

Failed Revenge

God yes: the days with her had been wonderful, and they were supposed to continue—those days; but she said good-bye and it's finished and over, and she behaved precisely the way he had begun it all: "Let's enjoy a few good days together! Nothing before and nothing after, but these few days should be good!" And that's just how they had been: wonderful, very very wonderful. So good, as a matter of fact, that he couldn't comprehend at all what she was saying: "Good-bye and it's finished and over!" To him—to whom these days had seemed too short; too short of course precisely because it was she who had anticipated what usually he was wont to say after a few days: "Good-bye and it's finished and over!" And now, after the last desperate sleepless night they sat in his car and drove back to the city to the house where she lived and both felt the fatigue creeping from their hot skin into their hearts, and it was very oppressive in the city and they smelled the exhaust fumes of the cars and tasted the dust and soot of the city on their tongues and when he had to stop at a red light he gave her a cigarette and took one himself, but after two puffs she threw it out the window and said: "No, I don't want one, it wears me down." He drove on and they spoke of the stupidity of letting cigarettes wear one down, and suddenly—and she said: "Now you look totally different: happy, satisfied, proud!"—and suddenly he too threw his cigarette out and said: "Let's stop smoking! Not tomorrow, not on the next birthday, but today, now; this very second." And they promised each other: with a kiss and a handshake and a solemn oath. Then the gate of the house grated shut and he returned to his car and didn't start up, but reached for a cigarette and rolled the cigarette between his lips and leaned far back and blinked into the smoke and thought that she won't be rid of him so quickly after all, but rather that she would be intimately bound to him for quite some time: for as long, in any case, as she would have to think how good it would be to smoke a cigarette. The other possibility however, namely that she could throw herself upon her couch upstairs and could smoke a cigarette, inhaling very deeply, deep into her body: this possibility did not occur to him, the fool, at all.

Love's Labor's Lost

The young painter had not exactly asked him, but merely indicated that she felt like exhibiting her work now. He, of course, for he liked her and happened to be unattached at the moment, had immediately offered his services to arrange something for her: "Perhaps at the Ministry of Culture, perhaps at the Academy, perhaps at the Secession or some other private gallery. I know quite a few people in this business—something will turn up." On her behalf he had visited the Ministry of Culture, the Academy, the Secession, this and that gallery owner until, at last, he found one who was willing: to be sure only in exchange for half the costs of catalogues, posters, and printed invitations. She was pleased when she heard the news and suggested that they could receive the subsidy from the Industrial Endowment for Culture or from the Governmental Art Department. Unfortunately, however, she had no contacts there. He offered to talk to the Secretary of the Endowment and to the senior government official in the Art Department. And after he had put in several appearances and had made telephone calls, he did indeed obtain the money which the gallery owner had demanded. There were supposed to be around thirty paintings. He helped her select the paintings, he made her compliments, and he assisted her in mounting the paintings or framing them. Together they designed the catalogue, for which he wrote an introduction, and the poster and the invitation notices. And all this time he courted her and she was tremendously nice to him and eternally grateful. And nothing more. They were, after all, dreadfully busy. And in the midst of all this she wanted to finish an oil painting on which she was working during the day, while he was supervising the printing of catalogues, posters, and invitations. And during the evenings they pored over the lists of all those she was meaning to invite. He typed the addresses for her and gave her a lot of other names of people who absolutely were to attend, and they spent several days in the gallery hanging the pictures and labeling them. And then the wines and drinks had to be prepared. And then it had arrived: the opening day of the art exhibit. Now there were repeated hand kisses and handshakes and countless beautiful words and most of the time he acted like a bodyguard and stood close by her and rejoiced over every word of praise concerning her that he had occasion to hear: he regarded the exhibit as if it were his own. And then, when the people had dispersed in the hall in front of the pictures, he kissed her hand, he kissed it for quite some time, almost too long in front of so many people, and finally when he raised his head, the critic of the *Express*, whom he knew slightly, stood before him and extended his hand and said: "It was tremendously nice of you to have been such a great help to my good friend. I myself never would have been able to do that. The entire world would have suspected me of doing that for, well, for personal reasons. Do you understand?" He managed to mutter: "Yes, yes, yes. I understand completely." Of course he did not understand yet. She, in the meantime, took the critic's arm, leaned on his shoulder, gazed up at him with her huge, round, blue, innocent eyes beneath a reddish-blond, bleached mop of hair, and spoke through moist lips: "Yes, darling, it was indeed tremendously nice of him. We really must be very grateful to him. God knows what people would have said! And I'm convinced: he understands." Now, to be sure, he understood. A little late, of course, for a man of almost forty.

The Blue Thistle of Romanticism

The man was walking away from the beach with his friend and spoke with him about things he never could have discussed with women. They walked along the shore and across the peninsula to the other shore and then followed the shore as far as the ruins, which they had often seen from afar but never up close. And there among the rocks the man discovered a blue thistle with six- and seven- and eight-fold serrated blossoms as narrow and as sharp as spears. He found the thistle very pretty, and he plucked it to bring to his wife. Yet he kept on talking with his friend and said to him: "Who am I finally: am I still I when I am thinking that something is happening to me which has not yet happened and probably never will happen? Am I now he to whom it is happening or still the one to whom it is not happening? Or am I both simultaneously, or neither of the two?" And so they spoke all during the very long walk about things he never could have discussed with women, and he was still holding the thistle, and then, while they drank a glass of wine in a restaurant close to the bungalow where they lived, they were still speaking of these things. Then they walked on and very soon arrived at the house, and there she stood in a white apron and a little red dress, the wife of the man who had plucked the thistle, stood there on her toes in the grass and took down the bathing suits from the clothes line, and when he saw her the man realized that he had left the thistle lying on the terrace of the restaurant. He was ashamed, and he said to his wife: "I wanted to bring you something and I did bring it almost as far as here and then I left it lying in the restaurant where we stopped." She burst out laughing and said: "That's easy to say!" He was still standing, but inwardly he had already gone back to the restaurant, and so, although he no longer felt like going, after her reply, he turned around and walked back to the restaurant, to fetch the thistle. It was a very short walk, but it seemed very long to him and therefore he walked quickly. He thought he should not have talked so much of all those things, then this would not have happened to him. And then he thought it was useless to return and fetch the thistle, because if he had left the thistle lying there, there must have been a reason for it; and he searched for this reason and he thought, he simply left the thistle there in order not to be exposed to danger and the suspicion of a lie. He thought it would have been the most banal lie of all if he had brought her the thistle. But since he had carried the thistle all this way and close to the destination, but not quite to the destination: therefore the thistle had become important to him. And therefore he walked even faster,

and he arrives at the restaurant, and there on the table the thistle still lies; he lifts it up and also lifts his eyes, and in his vision stands the waitress who earlier brought them the wine, and not until now does he notice her white teeth, when she laughs, gleaming from out of her full-bodied lips, and as he sees her, he knows: the thistle belongs only to her, and it was therefore that he had left it lying here, and he gives her the thistle and plunges into her laughter, into the midst of the white teeth of this divine animal,

yet he still wasn't there yet and walked faster and faster,

and then arrives at the restaurant, and there at the wall stands a woman and twists the thistle in her hand and gazes at the thistle and then at the man beside her and then casts an appraising glance at him, who had plucked the thistle and carried it on the long walk, but she believes that the man beside her did it, and therefore smiles at the man and gives him her hot hand on the stone wall, and soon it will be more than just her hand, and everything in return for this thistle, which not the man beside her, but he himself had plucked and carried here,

still he had not yet arrived and walked faster than ever before,

and then arrives at the restaurant, and this thistle, which he carried for so long, is no longer to be found anywhere: not on the table and not on the chair and nowhere else, and one day later he sees it again, in his wife's bedroom, and she received the thistle from a man who found it on the terrace and who didn't pluck it himself and didn't carry it on the long walk, who merely found it and gave it to her, and she took it and placed it next to her bed,

and therefore he was running now, because the thistle was important to him as nothing else in the world; it was his hope, his chance: it seemed appropriate to him for redeeming precisely the reason why he had left it lying there. He rushed upstairs and to the table which was already cleared, but under the chair, blue above the gray cement, lay the thistle, and hastily he seized the thistle and hurried back to the house and gave it to the woman, and the woman took the thistle and stuck it in one of the empty Tuborg bottles of sea-green glass; for she had a very great fondness for all that bloomed, and three days later she was no longer with him. Then the man, too, left the place, and other summer guests arrived; and one of them took the Tuborg bottle, with its spiky gray scrub in which the water had evaporated, and threw it into the garbage can and murmured something about typical Balkan sloppiness.

The Fall

He spent the summer with his uncle, the local parish priest, and Louise was also there this summer. She was a niece of the uncle's, who, however, was not his mother's brother but rather her cousin, and he did not manage to find out to what degree he was related to her. Yet every day they played together and were friends, and that was much more important to both of them. Whenever they were in the forest they stalked deer: first they stuck a finger in their mouth and held it up to discover the direction of the wind. They carved flutes and whistles from hazelnut wood and once they even went grape-stealing together. They had also smoked together and chewed chestnut leaves afterwards so that no one would detect the tobacco smell at home. In the poultry yard they shot sparrows and then counted who had gotten more; afterwards they dug a grave and planted a cross on the little hill, surrounded it with white pebbles and covered it with many flowers. Often they were allowed to ride along on the ladder wagon, and one of the hired men occasionally let them ride a horse. They learned how to lead a team of oxen, milk the cows, and mow the grass. They were there when the meadow beyond the big road was drained, near the stream where they caught fish with their bare hands. They also tried it with handkerchiefs, which they stretched with net-like wire beneath a rod, but they never caught anything with the handkerchief. On another day, wading in the stream up to their knees, they built a dam out of stones and sticks and sand, and then a good thirty steps further up, a second one, and guided the water out into the meadow. However, even in the dry area between the two dams they didn't find a single fish. Whenever it rained they played dominoes in the living room or they helped the maid in the kitchen with the potato peeling. They also read a great deal. In the parsonage there was a big book, as large as a newspaper, with stories about the Franco-Prussian War and containing very many drawings of the battles: defenders behind a cemetery wall, riders on the attack, a trumpeter hit in the chest, horses rearing in the mud before a cannon, a general on the commandeering hill, burning villages and bearded men on barricades with flags. They liked this book better than all other books.

On Sunday they went to mass and took communion, and if he also went to mass during the week—for he was an altar boy—Louise accompanied him to church. They also went to benediction, and sometimes they would go alone to church—it was, after all, a spot even more mysterious than any other: more so than the abandoned signalman's cabin or the shut down railroad tracks where one still could turn the rusty cranks and pull the rattling chains and pretend one was lowering the gates and at any moment the train from Hamburg to Rome would pass with elegant people leaning against the window and waving. They went to church very often, and once again they were alone in the church. Louise had a little sack of candies with her and she gave him a candy and took one herself and put it in her mouth. He was still holding the sticky candy in his hand and whispered: "In church one must not eat, that's a sin." She stuck her tongue out and the candy was protruding from her lips and she whispered, just as softly: "But there's nothing wrong with sucking it." He looked at her skeptically because he had never thought about that before. He also didn't quite know what to do with his candy. And since Louise didn't say another word he quickly slipped it into his mouth. They sat in a pew in front of the pulpit, and the church around him grew very dusky and suddenly very cold and it smelled of incense, and red and blue beams of light, flickering and vibrating, streamed from the colored windows. The banner which he had carried during the procession stood erect and huge in the middle of the room, and from all the altars, from all the paintings and from the ceiling the saints looked down upon him quizzically. He knelt down and prayed and he did not feel good with the candy in his mouth. But she had said that it was not a sin and therefore he held the candy in his mouth and tried not to bite on it. And he was very happy when they finally left the church. They walked down the big road and waited for a car. Several cars passed, one right after the other, and one came from the opposite direction, and they discussed what kind of car they would like to have one day. Then they went home and plucked a chicken and helped in the kitchen: it was like always. But still: he had to look at her, again and again, very furtively, and had to ask himself whether it was with her that he had stalked deer and stolen grapes, had carved flutes and dammed the stream. He didn't know what the matter was, and he continued to go sparrow-shooting with her, and he smoked with her and rode a horse with her and went to church with her. But he had to look at her constantly and no longer quite understood, and didn't know what the matter was, but only that it no longer was the same.

A Detour to Happiness

Actually she was a bit too thin for his taste, and that was the real reason why his love for her had subsided, and soon it subsided so much, in fact, that she, starved for affection, acquired a lover on the side. But the only time of day that she could visit him was the very early afternoon, right after lunch with her husband, and since the lover was full of good intentions he always invited her for a meal before they got down to business. Thus she had to eat lunch twice a day, and since these meals continued for several months she gained weight. She even grew somewhat plump—something that her husband perceived not merely with amazement (unsuspecting to be sure) but also with joy, so that joyfully he loved her again, loved her, in fact, as he had previously only loved his dream of a woman, and so soon she in turn found she no longer required her lover after all.

To Die and Yet to Live

When she reached her middle fifties and no longer was as young as one was supposed to be when one still wants to derive pleasure from it all, she said laughingly: "I'm now withdrawing into private life." Ten years later, however, she felt too old for everything, and because she didn't want to come to a slow and arduous end, she decided to withdraw completely from life: but by no means with a slap or a bang, but quietly, and imperceptibly—not merely to others but also to herself. She walked down to the beach in her bathingsuit which she wore underneath her summer-dress, threw the dress into the bushes, slid into the water, and swam out into the sea with still powerful strokes and kicks, from the shallow bay toward the misty, dusky horizon. She did not think; not even how long it might take. She did nothing but swim: swim with powerful strokes and kicks out into the sea, from the shallow bay toward the misty, dusky horizon. She did not think; she only stroked with her arms and kicked her feet and dove snortingly with her face into the water and raised it gasping for air, again and again, frequently, apparently endlessly, because she didn't count, she merely swam, and from her skin to her heart she was nothing but this act of swimming: this extending of arms and straddling of legs and this rowing of arms and clashing of legs and this angling of arms and crouching of legs, heavily breathing in the water and eyes at water level: when suddenly one of her knees struck sand with a crunching sound and the other knee hit against rocks and she lost her rhythm and lay on her stomach, barely twenty steps from the shore where people were splashing and throwing balls and swaying on air mattresses, somewhere far far away from the beach which she had just left an unimaginably long time ago, in order not to land anywhere anymore. She knelt, raised herself up, and shakily trudged to the shore, like a few others on her left and right, who had taken a little swim.

A Divine Judgment, of Sorts

He had just made himself comfortable in the taxi when his left hand fell upon something that was not the polyester upholstery of the seat. The object was smooth, flat and square: an envelope, sealed and somewhat thicker and less pliable than an ordinary letter. He held it in his hand and was about to hand it over to the taxi driver when he read—and he read it only because this letter looked markedly different from any other—he read, instead of an address, the typewritten sentence on the envelope: "To the man who finds this letter."

That was, quite unequivocally, he. And therefore he did not even pretend to have pulled the letter from his pocket but rather he tore it open at once, and shook out a few photos together with a typewritten sheet of paper. Of course he looked at these pictures first—because what he saw of a woman he rather liked: no face, admittedly, only her hair and neck and everything else; yes, everything else. He studied the photos and he realized that for quite some time he'd been very much alone; and when the taxi rattled over the railroad tracks and the photos slipped from his hand and fell to the floor, he fished for them and looked at them again, and then he read the letter. No return address, no signature; but everything else was clearly specified: place and time and signs of identification, and so forth.

A few hours later, precisely at nine in the evening and with a book in his left hand, he entered the Café Miramare and he could have recited this letter by heart. He walked past the bar, through a curtain made of strands of pearls into an adjoining room and as far as the alcove immediately behind the telephone booth. And there she sat—with a cognac and soda and two packs of Peer cigarettes on the table in front of her; there she sat in a red jersey dress with a white artificial flower pinned to it—and it was his wife. She jumped up, and infinitely slowly she smiled an agonizing smile and said: "You? What a surprise!" He said almost the same words, and then they were silent for a while. Finally she pointed to a chair opposite her and sat down again. He seated himself in the fauteuil and at the same time clamped the book into the back of his chair. Suddenly she smiled a different smile and asked: "Are you reading anything good?"

"Oh, well," he replied, pulled the book out from his back and placed it on the table so that he himself could read the title, "as you can see: about termites."

"Since when are you interested in termites?" It sounded like a reproach, and he said, "A friend recommended it to me and I wanted to browse in it."

"Here, in the café? At home you'd have it a lot more comfortable."

"At home," he said, "you know that the painters are at home at the moment."

"Now, at nine in the evening?"

"Of course not now, but during the day and therefore it's quite uncomfortable at home."

"But we just had everything painted, just before you threw me out; that's barely half a year ago."

"I can have painters over whenever I feel like it," he said unintentionally loudly, and even more loudly: "And moreover I did not throw you out; you ran off."

"Nonsense!" she said.

"You talk nonsense!" he cried. She looked around at the other tables and he looked around briefly and then said softly but very insistently: "Let's leave that aside and let's speak plainly! What kind of idiocy is this?"

"Excuse me?" she asked in a friendly tone.

"This idiotic behavior!"

"I don't know what you are talking about," she said in a somewhat less friendly tone.

He bit his lips and with abrupt, angular gestures he pointed to her dress and flower, to the cognac and soda, and seized the two packs of Peer and slammed them on the table. At the moment the waiter approached and took their order and then it was silent at their table. Only after he had gotten his beer he said: "Nude photos and such a letter—what a disgrace!" He shook his head vehemently as if reacting to something incomprehensibly stupid, but she only shrugged her shoulders very briefly. "Perhaps it makes no difference to you," he continued, "but it does make a difference to me; after all, we're still married."

"Only *de jure*, only in name," she replied.

"And what about this letter!" He shook his head again. "What is this supposed to mean: 'I set no conditions?'"

"It's supposed to mean exactly what it says."

"Does that mean you didn't want to ask for any money?"

"Swine!"

"What about you?" He raised his glass, in which the foam had settled, to his lips and set it down again without having taken a drink: "Really, I never would have expected this of you! How can you degrade yourself like this? Damn, what a disgrace!" He almost emptied his glass and had to cough.

"I was quite simply very much alone," she said as if to herself, and then to him, to his face red from coughing: "And you know what I never would have expected from you?"

"What?"

"That you would respond to such a letter and such photos—," but he interrupted her: "That's different. I'm a man. But you, as a woman, should be ashamed!"

"But I wasn't ashamed."

"That's just what I'm saying." Since she was silent he grew angry: "You took this approach because no one would look at you otherwise."

"And you came here because you wouldn't dare otherwise." He wanted to reply but she didn't give him a chance. "You thought you'd have it easy, you wouldn't have to bow and scrape for long, it would cost neither time nor money, and you'd certainly not be rejected, you coward!"

"I could have pretended to have come into the café by accident," he said with an indifferent shrug. She smiled indulgently, took his book out of his hand, and gently rapped it against his forehead a few times. He merely moved lamely, like a sleeper who wants to chase away a bothersome fly; and only after the book rested on the table again he said: "Let's stop talking about it. It's too stupid to talk about." She however asked: "I would like to find out why you came."

"Why do you think? Because I've been alone."

"I'll tell you why you came."

"All right, why?" He shoved his face into his glass of beer.

"You recognized me in the photos." He set his glass very awkwardly on the table, it fell over, a little beer ran across the marble, and then he finally said: "No."

She said: "Surely you must have recognized me."

"No, I swear it!" And he looked at her. But she was wiping the beer from the table top with her napkin and said, "Really, I was sure you recognized me."

"In these photos? Taken with shadows and against the light and retouched?" Hurriedly he searched for the pictures and gave them to her, and after she had examined each one she said: "Maybe you're right." Irresolutely she held the pictures in her hand, and when he reached for them she returned them without hesitating and later asked: "Do you want them?"

He did not place them in the envelope at once but twisted them in his fingers and said: "Do you want them back?"

"No, no," she said, "you can keep them if you like."

"No," he said, "not if you want them?"

Since she did not answer, he returned the photos to the envelope lying in front of him. The waiter came, he waved to him with his glass and the waiter brought another beer and left. She drank her cognac and said: "Please order me another one." He ordered the cognac and drank his beer and then said: "So, what are you doing now?"

"What do you think I'm doing?" she replied.

"I think I'll have another beer," he said after a while. She said nothing, he ordered the beer, and later he ordered another cognac for her. "Yes," she asked suddenly, "what is it that I should do now?" He raised his glass in order to read the slogan on the beer mat, turned the mat over and placed his glass on it again. She leafed through the book which was still lying before him on the table and said, without looking at him: "Don't let this lie here, please!"

"What? Oh, the photos." He slid the envelope into the breast pocket of his jacket and asked her: "Do you want another cognac?"

She said: "Maybe," and he drank another beer, and so it was midnight by the time they finally got home. She said: "I don't see any painters."

He said: "Let's not talk about it anymore."

Punt e Mes

They had been sitting on the now rapidly cooling rocks of the dam, which separated the shut-down salt pits from the open sea, just beside the colorfully painted wooden shack which was almost like a café during the summer months, where one could get Turkish coffee and ice and beer and fruit juice and where one could relax in the shade, because on the dam there were no trees, only shrubs and trampled grass. He had already been in Strunjan once before during the summer, amidst very many people who were lying here in the sun, chewing their *Schmalzbrote* and talking on about what they had talked about at home. Now it was Easter and he had come here because he wanted to be all alone; and he had been certain that he would be all alone, for in April no one came to such a place where one can't do anything else but swim. When he arrived he had indeed been the only guest, but on the following day already other guests came, thirty from one and twenty from another bus, and several with their own cars. He said to Victor, who was managing the hotel and the bungalows: "Victor, this is impossible! I've got to think something over, therefore I've got to be alone. Tomorrow I'm leaving." Victor explained to him what was happening: a kind of conference: students and professors: from here and from Austria, Germany, Italy: archaeologists. He said to Victor: "But I'm not an archaeologist, damn it! I'm a man who has to contemplate something important, and therefore I'm driving over to Krk tomorrow." He sat in the taproom, in the front, where the music box was standing, at a table next to the bar, and drank his wine, and the archaeologists sat in the dining room, in the back, and had their dinner. Local men stood at the bar, and occasionally one of them walked over to the music box, threw in a coin, pressed the knobs and returned to the others. The men selected only Slovenian songs. Then the waitress emerged from behind the bar and selected the American hit which happened to be popular here at the time; and one of the men danced with her. Victor asked what it was that he had to think about, and he answered: "Whether I should get a divorce." Victor felt that as long as one was still thinking about it, it wasn't a serious problem. He told Victor: "It was only a joke. I'm thinking about something else: I'd like to discover a card game that leaves nothing to luck, but rather comes out even, must come out even, as long as one doesn't make a mental error. Do you follow me?" He stared into Victor's gray face, into gray eyes beneath his thinning gray hair, and he continued to stare after him when Victor was pushing the empty tables against the wall to make room for the couples who were coming from the dining room in the back to the front, to the taproom. He was annoyed that he had mentioned it to Victor: to someone who never let on what he understood or did not. Ill-humored he walked over to the music box, selected a song he liked, and suddenly he sensed that someone was looking over his shoulder. He moved aside and asked the girl: "Which song are you looking for?"

She said: "Oh, I'm sure they don't have here what I'm looking for."

He asked her: "Tell me anyway."

She said: "'Petite fleur.'"

He had to collect himself somewhat before he could calmly reply: "That's just what I have selected."

She laughed: "No!"

"But yes! For us. To dance." The arm in the music box lowered the record with a tinny hum, the needle descended and they danced. Afterwards they drank a glass of wine at the table near the bar. The girl was called Anna and came from Germany, but she was studying in Rome. He said "Annnna" to her, with a long N as only Italians would say. They danced again and later on other people joined them at their table. Finally, after Victor locked up, the professor from Zagreb and a girl by the name of Nelly, from Austria, who was also studying in Rome like Anna, went with them, up to his bungalow room and drank the wine he had and talked for a long time about many things. Around midnight the professor left and then Nelly left and Anna went with her. It hadn't even occurred to him to ask her to stay with him in his room.

The following morning during breakfast he was alone: two buses had taken the archaeologists to Pula. He drank a schnapps and went out onto the dam to swim. The water was cold, but not any colder than the Danube was in the middle of summer. When he had swum far out, he swallowed a mouthful of water. Later, on the dam, he leaned against the boards of the shack heated by the sun and smoked a couple of cigarettes. At noon he lunched alone on the large terrace. Victor did not bother to ask him when he was leaving. The archaeologists did not return until very late from Pula. He ate dinner with Anna, with Nelly and with the professor inside in the dining room.

On the following days too he was alone, because every morning the buses arrived and beckoned the archaeologists with their honking to the Istrian antiquities. In the afternoons they returned home and after their snack they stayed on the terrace and listened to the lecture of one of the professors. He listened to all these lectures and chose a seat so that he could observe Anna taking notes. On one of the evenings he drove to Piran with her, to a night club; there they drank champagne from Bakar and danced a lot. While dancing his face touched hers; she liked it. On the following evening when he did the same in Strunjan in front of all the others: she liked it still.

Easter Sunday they had off: no outing and no lecture. They had a late breakfast and he was lingering with her for a long time at the bar. She said: "They don't have Punt e mes here."

He asked: "What's that?"

She said: "Something that I like very much."

"A schnapps?"

"More like wine than schnapps. A bitter vermouth. An aperitif." She walked to the music box and played "Petite fleur." When she returned to the bar he said: "We can't dance now. But we could go swimming."

She said: "It's too cold."

He said: "It's not too cold."

She said: "And besides, I don't have my bathing suit with me." But then she hit upon the idea of borrowing a bathing suit from the waitress. The waitress said: "Brr, it's so cold."

She said: "I'm sure it's not too cold." Then they walked to the dam and swam out a ways. Then he called to her: "Take a sip of water!"

"Why?"

"The people here say that it helps one's digestion and creates an appetite. It is," and he took a sip of the water, "also a kind of aperitif."

She laughed: "But not a Punt e mes!" He had swum very close to her and swallowed another mouthful in front of her. She stuck out her tongue, to taste the water, and cried: "O awful, that's terrible!"

He said: "If you drink it intentionally, willingly, consciously: then it doesn't taste bad." She looked at him incredulously, but then took a sip and said: "You are right, it doesn't taste so bad. I thought it would taste terrible." Leisurely they floated on their backs back to the shore, and on the dam they dried off on the hot, sun-drenched wooden boards. They were alone out here. He said: "You were very brave."

She looked at him and asked: "Why?"

"With the water." She only laughed and he continued: "Actually you have earned yourself a Punt e mes."

"But they don't have any here."

"Surely we'll find one somewhere; we'll just look." They walked back to the hotel and to his car. They drove to Buje, Novigrad, Poreč and nowhere did they find Punt e mes; in Rovinj too there was none. She said: "It's not that important. But at home, if you still think of it, will you drink a Punt e mes, yes?"

"But it is very important," was all he said. They drove back to Poreč, to an outdoor garden restaurant right next to the tiny harbor, and after dinner she plucked several branches of laurel growing all over the restaurant garden. He asked: "Whom do you wish to crown?"

She said: "One can use it for soups and sauces or add it to lentils . . . ." She threw the branches into a gutter and spoke of the excavations south of Poreč which they had visited on Friday. It was very hot in the car and they rolled down both windows; the map rustled on her knees in the draught. He showed her a few more spots in Istria: Pazin and Motovun and several others. Suddenly he said: "Portorož," and slapped his forehead. "In Portorož we'll get it!" At the bar of the "Riviera" they counted nine different whiskeys, but there too Punt e mes was not to be had. They ate on the quay in Piran, outdoors, at one of the tables surrounding the charcoal grill and then they drove back to the hotel. They got out of the car and walked out onto the dam and there they sat for a long time, very close together, almost entwined, on the rapidly cooling rocks. Along the horizon dusk spread out above the lighter sea like a very high, steep and dark shore, and several little lights of boats, resembling houses along the beach, stood out. And she had said: "If you look continuously you don't realize that they are moving." After a while, however, one of the little lights had vanished and later on they saw another light vanishing and then a third one, and each one appeared to vanish at a spot very close to them at the other end of the shallow bay of Strunjan where the gentle contour of the high land of the peninsula near the citadel broke off and fell abruptly into the sea like a wall. And then, the last of the little lights swam in the now solely deep gray-blue of water and night like a lonely mirrored, totally forgotten star. They did not take their eyes off and it did not seem to move, and suddenly it vanished. In his hand he felt her heart beating and he felt her shivering. He took off his pullover and placed it around her shoulders and said: "In seven years I won't know anything about you any more, and then when we meet again I won't recognize you any longer. But until my death I shall remember these lights before the shore of dusk, like lights of houses along the beach, and how they wandered imperceptibly and vanished, one after the other, vanished along this wall." Nothing else was said. She noticed how he too was shivering now. They rose and returned to the hotel. There had been a few more days: dancing in the evenings cheek to cheek in the tap room, a few drinks of schnapps at this or that bar, hot hands clutched together under the table, soft conversations with long, very long pauses, and then one day the archaeologists did not depart early one morning but remained sitting in the dining room: the professors gave their final lecture, and then suitcases were packed and addresses exchanged. Toasts were buzzing above the lunch table: in German, Italian, Slovenian, Croatian, even in Latin, and Victor was dragging a big package to the table, the Germans tore it open, it was filled with Bavarian beer mugs which they now passed out amidst hellos and laughter. Anna said to him: "That's why I don't live in Germany."

He said: "You are too severe."

She said: "Probably." And after a pause: "I would like a different souvenir." He looked at her and she spoke very softly, almost timidly: "Your map of Istria, the one we studied while driving around here." He walked down to the parking lot and from the car he took the map which was still lying unfolded on the passenger seat and gave it to her. She said cheerfully now: "I also have something for you." It was the record they played and danced to here: "Petite fleur." "I bargained with Victor and talked him out of it." He pressed her hand briefly and very firmly and then the bus honked downstairs:

terribly loudly. Their lips touched: hurriedly and in passing—very much like down which a bird loses in flight when it brushes against something; and as if with averted face. Everyone was crowding down the stairs, corners of suitcases were shoved into the hollows of knees, Victor was fighting with the gesticulating driver; and someone waving a bag called: "Who has forgotten this? Who has forgotten this bag?" And someone else said: "That's the bus for the people from Germany and Austria." Anna inquired of Victor and Victor said that the bus to Italy would not come for another ten or fifteen minutes. And so they stood upstairs again on the terrace, leaning on the banister and staring into the dirty gray of the cement floor. Finally she said: "You know, the conference was actually very interesting."

He asked: "So you found it worthwhile?"

"Yes. Very definitely. It was the best of all the conferences I've attended so far."

"Yes. I'm happy for you." He took a cigarette from his case, rolled it between his fingers and then put it back with the others. "I don't know much about it, as you realize, but somehow I got the impression that it was very interesting for all of you."

She said: "There were some very good people here."

He said: "Yes. The professor from Zagreb."

"And Antonioni."

"Yes, Antonioni."

"And also the lecturer from Graz."

"Was she nice?"

"Yes, very!"

He turned very abruptly towards her and implored her sharply and beseechingly: "Let's stop this pretense, please!"

She said very softly: "Forgive me!"

He said: "Anna!" She looked at him and he whispered: "Please stay!" She only shook her head very slowly. And he asked: "Why not?"

She said: "Tomorrow I have to be at the Institute again."

"The Institute will get along without you if you don't return until the day after tomorrow."

She said: "I can't."

He pleaded: "Just this one night."

"I have to get back."

"I'll take you to Rome in my car; by noon you'll be at the Institute."

She said: "Try to understand me!"

He said: "God, I don't even understand myself!"

"I—I think I understand you a little."

He looked at her and said very calmly: "Anna, I've been a fool: until now I did not know how much I love you."

"But I," she said, "I realized it."

He said again: "I've been a fool," but she interrupted him: "You mustn't think that you alone have a monopoly on foolishness." The sun splashed its light onto the multicolored bright walls of the bungalows; from the kitchen he heard the rattling of plates and cups; over there was Nelly fumbling around in her suitcase; and very far away he saw a little dot of the sea where they had swum. He pulled out a cigarette and said: "Anna, let's go and have a drink!"

She laughed a little: "Punt e mes is not to be had here."

He said: "Yes, that's true."

She said: "But at home when you drink a Punt e mes . . . ," but she could not finish the sentence.

He said: "And certainly not just then." The bus still had not arrived, and he asked her: "Is it a Spanish word?"

"No; Italian."

He asked: "It's an Italian vermouth?"

She said: "Yes. From around Turin."

He rolled the cigarette, which was not yet lit, between his fingers until it crumbled. "Too bad," he said then. "It's only thirty minutes from here to the border, and to Trieste perhaps fifty. We were driving in the wrong direction."

"No," she said, "no."

He took out a new cigarette, lit it with the lighter, and said: "You really are a brave girl."

She said: "Oh, let's not talk about me."

"About what else?"

She rested her temple against her index finger, and then said: "Let's talk about—Punt e mes!" He asked her the meaning of the name. "It's in dialect and means: A point and a half. They say that the name came into being about two hundred years ago: A few people there speculated with stocks, the stocks rose one and a half points, which they immediately celebrated, of course with their local wine, and out of gratitude for their luck they named the wine: A point and a half. Punto e mezzo. Punt e mes."

He said: "It's a nice story."

She said: "Se non è vero, è molto ben trovato." And continued: "It can be ordered without saying a word." She pointed one thumb into the air and with her other hand she cut horizontally across it. "In Italy that means: Punt e mes."

He saw the bus turning in from the main road, and he said: "You know my reason for having come here."

She said: "I know it."

"Basically," he said, "I came here to discover a card game which leaves nothing to luck but which comes out even, must come out even as long as one doesn't make a mental error. Do you understand?"

She said: "Yes."

"But it was my mistake to believe that there is such a thing."

She said, very quickly and almost pleadingly: "Take care, take care," turned away and ran to the stairs and ran down the stairs and climbed into the bus which had just now begun to honk, and he knew that she would neither turn around nor wave any more. He too did not wave, but went to his room, to which she had never returned after that evening with Nelly and with the professor, and which now struck him as emptier than even before. That same night still he had driven home, slowly, making detours, as if hesitating; with a mind full of questions. A Punt e mes he had found already before dinner, in Klagenfurt, and then at home he bought a whole bottle; and sometimes he played her record. He did his work and lived with his wife and children, and when he thought of Anna he was ashamed of the words he had spoken at night on the dam in the ocean; because it seemed impossible to him that he would ever forget her. He had worries and he also had luck, and time passed. He thought of Anna now entirely without pain: it had been, and now it was over. He still played the record now and then, until one of the children broke it completely. He was in Istria several times, even in Strunjan, and it was there that his children learned how to swim. He got a divorce and then had girl friends, he did his work and grew older. Of Anna he thought only rarely: he did not like to think of useless things. And then seven years had passed and suddenly he realized that he was hoping they would meet each other again; and shortly before Easter he even considered driving to Strunjan. He did not go after all because he feared that it was not a good idea to intervene in his own fate; but all these days he crisscrossed the inner city and occasionally drank a Punt e mes in espressos and bars and looked into many, innumerably many faces, and then realized suddenly: he would not recognize her anymore. Summer came and then autumn, and he tried to remember: there was Strunjan with gray Victor, who pushed the empty tables against the wall in the evenings, there were the laurel branches in the gutter, the honking buses, there was the lecturer from Graz, but there was no longer any recognizable Anna. There was "Petite fleur," cheek to cheek. There was Professor Antonioni. There was the Bakarska in Piran. There was a cigarette crumbled between his fingers. There too was Nelly, fumbling with her little suitcase. And no Anna. There was the hot, coarsely grained wood of the shack on the dam. The mouth filled with the taste of salt. The gaudy yellow bathing suit of the waitress. No Anna. Yet it was with her that he had sat on the rocks of the dam, they had seen the little lights vanishing, and these little lights he saw again now: resembling lights of houses along the shore of a very tall steep and dark coast. He forgot the professor from Zagreb, the charcoal-grilled meal, and the lectures on the terrace, but the little lights remained. Another year passed, and the little lights were still there. He forgot the beer mugs and the map rustling beside him, and he also forgot the hot, coarsely grained wood of the shack on the dam, the taste of salt in his mouth, the gaudy yellow bathing suit; and only the little lights he did not forget: their distant glow flooded over everything else that had been, and bore something unspeakably tender towards him that enveloped him, lifted him up, carried him away as if on waves, floated him back to that dam on whose cooling rocks they had sat then, very close together, almost entwined, and she had said: "If you look continuously you don't realize that they are moving." The tenderness was all round him, and he called it "Anna," and he spoke this name often to himself into the stillness of the room and toward the empty passenger seat in the car and into the crowds of people at five o'clock on the Graben and into the music he happened to be hearing. He said "Anna" and again "Anna" in order not to suffocate in all the tenderness, and then he once wrote her a letter: only a few lines, to her address in Rome of nine years ago now. He entertained little hope of reaching her there. He merely thought it was better than screaming.

He delved deeply into work, and sometimes he succeeded in no longer hoping for a reply. And one day his letter returned, the envelope covered with black and blue postmarks and red notations. He placed the letter in a new envelope, with the address of the Roman Institute which he managed to procure in Vienna. Weeks later this letter too was returned; but now that he had begun to search for her he dispatched his letter to still other addresses: he did not want to be cowardly again as he had been then, at Easter after seven years, when he did not, after all, drive down to Strunjan, where she perhaps had wished and longed for him. The letter returned again and again, and it also returned from the places in Germany where he supposed that she could have studied and lived at one time. He thought of Nelly, but it was very difficult to locate her because she had married; he located her in Weitra, as wife of a *Gymnasium* professor, and she still remembered him. Nelly tried the Institute, and that took a long time and then was fruitless as well. She still had one or two ideas, and he gave her the letter, and then he began to feel ridiculous. Occasionally he wished he had never written this letter; but Nelly was now mailing it for him and he was very grateful to her. He lived with those little lights, amidst something very tender: as if in a second skin. He lived as always, but drank almost nothing, only his Punt e mes every day. And then one day there was a voice on the telephone that told him: "I am here at the train station, but I think it would be better if I came to you because you would not recognize me any more."

He would not have recognized her again, it's true, and he admitted it to her. She said: "I would have recognized you for a thousand years." They were lying in bed and eating oranges and delighting in the juice spraying from the bursting skins and in the mornings they still smelled its scent in the pillows. They often spoke of Strunjan, and he said: "I was very foolish," but she interrupted him: "You were not foolish, you loved her."

He said: "Yes, and I admitted it to you."

She said: "You didn't even have to admit it."

He asked: "Was that the reason?"

She laughed: "Oh, no! I was still a little girl, then; I shuddered at the thought of losing my girlhood, just as I shuddered from the water. I was so afraid that would destroy everything." Her mouth became smaller as she then continued: "I did not know all the things that are destroyed nonetheless, and did not know where the destructions come from. Did not know that they never fail to appear, these destructions. Did not know that no one is spared. No one."

He pushed her tousled hair from her forehead and said: "You don't look like someone who's been worn down."

"I've never forgiven you for it," she said. Then she laughed again: "You must give me a thorough thrashing for my foolishness at the time."

He asked: "So, what is it then with your marriage?"

She said: "Laurels in soups and sauces."

He asked: "And that's not good?"

"That's just it," she exclaimed. He saw her toes curling as she continued: "It's precisely as one never believes it can be: completely normal. Horrible."

He said: "Luckily it's not me," and she said: "Yes, luckily!" They had endless fun together and they were satisfied. They did not talk much about Strunjan any more; when they listened to music, however, he said: "Guess what, the record is gone. The children played with it until it broke."

"Strange," she said. "Your map is gone too. A few years ago we were in the South, and in Trieste we were robbed: all our luggage was taken, and also your map." Then they spoke again of other things and were happy. He looked at her constantly, and he watched how she spread honey on her bread and how she pulled her nylons straight, how the words poured quickly from her pen and how she still reached for him just before falling asleep: he looked at her and compared her to something he no longer could remember. They never spoke about the little lights. Sometimes he still thought of the little lights; but he made an effort to think of them as little as possible: he did not like to think of useless things. Occasionally, when she was even more lovely than he realized, the little lights vanished; and once in the midst of their happiness, she asked: "Are you sad?"

He said: "No," and it was the truth. She also stayed with him the following week, and then she drove home: they waved to each other much longer than they were able to see each other. She was a splendid woman, and he thought of her very much, and he soon met her again and then more and more often. He loved her laughter, darkly clattering like her chain of amber, he loved the rosy balls of her narrow toes, he loved her heartbeat in his hand, and he loved all this like nothing else in the world. Now and then he remembered occasionally, full of wonderment, a gradually fading dream.

In Praise of Craftsmanship

There once lived in Vienna a poor locksmith apprentice, who was in love with his master's daughter and who was also loved by her. The aging master, who had no sons, was not opposed to their union, but he was not willing to consent to the marriage until the apprentice had passed the master exam. At the next opportunity already the young man, full of hope, yet trembling and perspiring on account of the double risk, attempted the exam and failed, of course. Whereupon the master proclaimed his intention of keeping him on in his workshop as an apprentice—for he was diligent and decent enough—but of giving his daughter in marriage to another man.

At this the apprentice fell into deep despair and thought of nothing else but his misfortune. In the evening, after work, he sat alone in a corner of the inn; during a game of cards he often started a quarrel; and he avoided the dance floor altogether. No sunshine sparkling on the waves of the Danube and no merry snowflakes at his window could cheer him up, no counsel could comfort him, no stroll in the Prater and no pleasures at the fairgrounds could distract him from his grief. He scorned even the tastiest dishes and he grew thin; but secretly he reached for the schnapps at all hours of the day. And he no longer dared to face his beloved and confess his sorrow. Silently he did his suffering and it consumed him until he was without any joy. And gradually the wish arose in him to end these sufferings—since they would not vanish—with his life. In sleepless nights, as he pressed his tear-filled eyes into the pillow and imagined his beloved before the altar with another, his thoughts dwelled on the well-known reports of all the various suicides which people had ever committed. He had no access to poison; therefore he eliminated poison at once. The hasty resolve to hurl himself from the highest window into the street was just as hastily dismissed: he was repelled by the thought of his shattered skull. For a stab into the heart or a cut through the throat or an artery, on the other hand, he lacked the final courage. Death in the water seemed too slow to him, especially since he was a very good swimmer and feared that he would resist going under. Hanging likewise seemed too agonizingly slow, and the idea of burning only made him shudder. A pleasant death, so he had often heard, is said to be freezing in the snow; but now it was April, and he could not wait until it was winter again. He would have liked to starve himself most of all, but it was probable that as soon as his condition was evident, he would be transported to a hospital and forcibly fed. The most reliable and at the same time least painful means to be released from all suffering, he told himself, would be without doubt a well-aimed shot into his chest; he found this idea of death especially appealing because as a young chap he had been a soldier for one year. Only pregnant servant girls choose death by drowning; only apprehended murderers hang themselves; only effeminate cowards take poison; a soldier, however, he concluded, dies by the bullet. But: he possessed no weapon. And no money to purchase one.

Meanwhile chance came to his rescue: his master had received a cheap load of scrap metal from a peddler and among various metallic material, which the apprentice had to sort for future use, there was a pistol; actually: a pistol barrel together with the most important parts of the mechanism. He could easily replace the missing parts. One of his former comrades who was now working in the arsenal supplied him, after a few glasses of wine, with the appropriate bullet. And then, late that night in his attic room he pressed the cold muzzle against his bared breast, uttered a brief prayer towards heaven and a very long sigh to his beloved, and groped for the trigger with his index finger as he had learned; whereby the muzzle slipped sideways between two ribs. He realized at once that since he was aiming the weapon at himself he would have to pull the trigger not with his index finger but rather with his thumb; however, the trigger guard was a bit too narrow for his strong thumb. He tried once more with his index finger; he wrenched his shoulder; and now he had a better grip on the unwieldy instrument. As he was about to shoot, it seemed to him that he had placed the muzzle too low under the heart; suddenly he lowered the hand that held the pistol and with his other hand he felt for his heartbeat. He located it, raised his pistol again, but was unsure whether the muzzle had found it. And besides, he saw his hand wet with perspiration and shaking spasmodically. And he knew: he was afraid. Not of dying; but of the shame of missing the fatal shot, of being merely wounded; of not being able to die but having to live on as an unsuccessful suicide. Once more he raised the weapon, which wavered wildly before him, and then he dropped his hand and sank down on his bed and shoved the pistol quickly under his straw mat and fell asleep at once and awoke again immediately and suddenly realized: he had to secure the pistol's muzzle in such a way that the bullet could not miss its target even if his hand failed. Then he fell asleep again and slept through the night.

After work the next day he stayed on alone in the workshop. From all the metal lying around he selected a strip three fingers wide, bent one end of it over his left shoulder and at the other end, precisely over his heart, he cut a hole to fit the muzzle of the pistol. The next evening he attached clamps so that the muzzle fitted firmly into the hole. Then he constructed a horizontal band around his body to prevent the contraption from sliding back and forth. In order to put this outfit on he had to attach two hinges under his shoulders as well as a clasp on his back; all this he constructed in the course of the following evenings. Finally, at the fitting, the apprentice, who was a pedantic worker, was so annoyed by the lack of symmetry of the contraption that he added a second brace over the right shoulder to complement the left, whereby the whole outfit sat perfectly firmly. By this time the muzzle of the pistol no longer pointed directly to the heart, but he adjusted it by altering the braces.

During the many fittings, to be sure, the inventor was very pleased with his contraption, but he had also experienced crushing, bruising pains on his shoulders and ribs and therefore he inserted padding occasionally beneath the cold and hard iron. The padding, however, slipped and the creases likewise pressed into his flesh and scraped his skin; the only solution was to pad the entire contraption on the inside: for this purpose the apprentice gathered the cuttings of very thick red velvet material which he sized and pasted and sewed on with the finest wire. Now it was virtually a pleasure to don the outfit; almost a titillating sensation, which the proud manufacturer wanted to enjoy to the fullest. But now he was greatly pained by the discrepancy between the delicately constructed interior and the coarse exterior. And thus he spent the following evenings decorating the exterior of his contraption and he derived daily new pleasures from the progress of his invention.

One evening, as he was sitting alone in the workshop, happily chiseling away at the contraption which had at one time been so rough, the master had invited the most noble members of the guild to his house to show and explain to them a new tool which he had ordered from England. After enjoying some wine they entered the workshop, precisely at the moment when the apprentice had donned the contraption for yet another fitting. When he saw the master and all the others he felt like sinking into the ground for shame, and he wished he were dead; which he could very easily have become by merely pulling the trigger. But precisely this thought did not occur to him because after all his labors he had forgotten to what purpose and end he had constructed this device. He had long since stopped sitting alone in the inn, music had long since made his legs tingle again, and schnapps had long since ceased to comfort him. More than once he had planned to beg his beloved for a talk and in that talk ask for her renewed trust. At the moment, of course, discovered and compromised, he regarded himself totally and irrevocably lost. But when his master's horror soon gave way to curiosity, and this curiosity turned into admiration, the apprentice was as pleased as he had been all along (though unrecognized as pleasure) during the construction of his device. Full of amazement and wonder at himself he told what had impelled him to build the device and how he had gone about it. But it was not so much from his words as from his invention, which all had approved by now, that the master learned of the great love of the poor apprentice and at the same time also of his great ability in the trade in which he had failed to attain the title of master. Among the gentlemen present there were also some who had examined him at that time before the guild and they said: "He has truly constructed a masterpiece of a most curious sort, and let us recognize it as such." In spite of this praise the apprentice insisted upon taking an appropriate examination and returned to his master with the best report. Thereupon the master offered his daughter to him in marriage and after he retired his son-in-law managed the workshop so successfully that the shop soon turned into a small factory which is still producing useful things today.

A Portrait of Man and Wife

After looking around the rather large dining hall of the "Hahnhof" in the Leopoldstrasse in Munich, they headed toward my window table and asked whether they could take a seat. I was chewing on a bit of ox meat, nodded affirmatively and pointed with my hand to the bench opposite me. The man nodded gratefully in turn; the woman raked me with an examining glance. With a small, yet still too grandiose a gesture he let the woman precede him, she pushed her way in, and he sat down beside her. They were both between forty and fifty, both a bit stocky and plump, and both were dressed as well, that is: as smartly as is possible if one shops in the best department store of a large city or if one resorts to the best tailor in a small city; perhaps they came from Kassel, perhaps from Siegen. I rather believe: from Siegen. And in any case they were people who feel they have to behave differently, that is, more refined and correctly in a strange large city than at home. The woman wore some jewelry, and both looked a little like children who had been bathed for confirmation, coiffured and squeezed into new, to be sure, but too tight, clothes.

Perhaps they had slept late and just now, shortly before noon, made their morning toilette: the barely noticeable stale scent of a bathroom still enveloped them. I asked myself whether they were married. He treated her a trace too courteously, in my opinion, to be married to her; but possibly he acted this way because they were not at home now but rather in a strange city and perhaps on vacation, or perhaps attending a conference; or simply because he was rather short and, at any rate, not a centimeter taller than she, and short men, to be sure, are not necessarily more courteous than tall ones, but they strike one as being more polite because they always have to look up, whereas the tall ones can always look down. That they were married, to each other, that is, I deduced from their dress: it was by no means the same, but wholly similar in regard to fashion, to substance and quality of material, to the tailoring: thoroughly middle class and one to two years out of date. I continued to ask myself what kind of car they could possibly have, and I was sure it was a rather recent model but not a Mercedes and just as unlikely a Volkswagen; most probably it had to be an Opel Rekord.

Meanwhile the waitress came and the man ordered—they must have agreed upon it beforehand—two *Metzelsuppen*; that happens to be a specialty in every "Hahnhof," but listed on the menu only on certain days. I personally don't like this particular soup, already because of its name;˙ but some people are absolutely crazy about it and look forward all week long to this one day when *Metzelsuppe* was served. Well, it didn't

---

˙A soup served on slaughter days; *Metzger* means butcher.

take long at all, and the waitress brought the two soups. The man reached for the spoon and waited, eagerly eyeing the woman, for her to start; simultaneously they brought their spoons to their lips. Then the man dipped his spoon into the bowl again in order to eat. The woman, however, after she had withdrawn the spoon from her mouth, stiffened and continued to hold the spoon in front of her chin like someone who has to swallow ghastly medicine. Her face which had resembled a rubber animal that had been blown up tightly for some time and whose air then had gradually been released—presumably she was on a diet—her face now collapsed into innumerable folds toward her mouth, as if a hole had been punched into said rubber animal. Then suddenly she dropped the spoon into her bowl and said, looking straight ahead: "There's something wrong with the soup." She did not even look at the man, but she said it in such a way as if she had discovered his intention to poison her with this soup.

The man, who was just about to derive visible pleasure from his second spoonful, came to an abrupt halt in his movement, glanced briefly and obliquely at the woman, cautiously tasted the soup and said somewhat anxiously: "You think so?"

She said: "There's definitely something wrong. It does not taste right."

The man said: "Yes," and tasted it again. "Yes. Yes yes. You're right, there's something wrong with the soup today."

She spoke sternly, threateningly, extortionately: "Totally spoiled."

He slid the spoon once more into his mouth, tested the contents of the soup, and said, after he had swallowed the soup, very eagerly: "Yes, you're right, this time the soup is definitely not quite in order." I knew now that they were married and shortly before had had a fight. None of this interested me in the least, but they were sitting at my table, after all, and I heard him saying: "It tastes like—I don't know what, today."

"It tastes spoiled, that's what it tastes like. "

"Yes, really." And: "I'm terribly sorry."

She said: "I have no intention of eating this soup." Startled, he looked at her for a very brief moment and was about to say something else and then perceptibly said nothing after all—which always strikes me as much dumber than even the dumbest utterance. And she, of course, immediately cut in: "We have to make a complaint." And she pushed her soup bowl, together with the spoon, over to him, thereby charging him with the complaint, and he, reacting like a billiard ball that has been hit by another, pushed his own bowl toward the edge of the table, and I could tell how desperately he would have liked to eat the soup. She, however, said: "We have to make a complaint," and therefore he pushed the bowl even closer to the edge of the table. Other than that he did nothing, and she ordered him to call the waitress. He called for the waitress and complained: he spoke with a calm voice and totally harmless words, and the waitress too spoke quite calmly and said that she would bring, if that was their wish, two new bowls of soup. She took the bowls from the table and hurried away, and she returned with two other bowls and new spoons, and the man and the woman ate the soup after they had tasted it, as hastily as their dignity permitted; and all the while they discussed the other soup. She said: "I noticed it at once; with the first spoonful I noticed it already," and he said: "Yes, it was noticeable immediately, with the first spoonful already," and they emptied their bowls and then wanted to pay. The waitress came and she figured not two but rather four bowls of soup. The man did not say anything and was about to pay when he suddenly felt the woman's glance, like a hand, on his billfold; and he said: "Yes, but the soup—we only ate—the first soup, we didn't even—there was something wrong with it;" "it was spoiled," the woman corrected him, "it was spoiled," the man said, "and therefore we didn't eat it, but had to send it back." There was a brief dispute in which the woman did not participate so much with words as with her look, which grasped the man by the neck like a clawed fist. The waitress went to get the business manager, and meanwhile the woman said to the man: "We have no intention of paying for the spoiled soup. Or do you perhaps intend to pay for the spoiled soup?" The man assured her that he had no intention of doing so, and he fidgeted nervously with his billfold. And then the business manager, a tall, good-looking man of about sixty who was limping with one leg, appeared behind the waitress. The business manager was very polite and listened to all the man had to say and then replied: "But that's not possible at all because the other bowls came from the same large pot, and I myself have just tasted it and no one else has made a complaint; so that's just not possible." The man told the entire story a second time, and he said, turning to the woman: "With the first spoonful already my wife noticed that there was something wrong with the soup, and I also noticed it immediately." He had evidently hoped that the woman would now come to his aid; but she remained silent; she did not even nod her head, and therefore the man said to the business manager, who was now disagreeing with him more sharply: "This gentleman here," and with a beseeching gesture implying both apology and assistance, he pointed to me, "this gentleman here surely saw that with the first spoonful already we noticed: no, there's something wrong with this soup, with the first spoonful already, and both of us agreed." And with the utmost struggle he added: "And totally independently of each other." Everyone looked at me, only the woman looked beyond me, and I thought: perhaps there was a hair in her soup, or something had fallen or dropped into her bowl in the kitchen, that can happen, and actually because I did not want to abandon the man I said: "Yes, I did indeed notice that the lady and gentleman were already dissatisfied with the first spoonful." These words gave the man a little encouragement, and he said to the business manager: "Well, you see: with the first spoonful already." The business manager now declared decidedly that he could not honor this complaint, and repeated briefly and precisely his reasons for it; while speaking he moved his flat hand and bent arm back and forth horizontally like a saw in front of his chest; otherwise his massive body remained motionless. And now the man pressed and squeezed out his story for the third time and turned again and again to his right, to the woman, who still did not say anything; her face was puffed up, as if full of words, but she said nothing at all, and so the business manager had won. He now interrupted the man, and with a final jolt of his sawing flat hand he cut the thread of the story and demanded the payment for all four bowls of soup. With trembling fingers the man reached for his billfold and with a voice whose redeeming cry was stifled by the cudgel of embarrassment: "We have repeatedly eaten *Metzelsuppe* here, and we have eaten *Metzelsuppe* in the 'Hahnhof' in Düsseldorf and in the 'Hahnhof' in Frankfurt and in the 'Hahnhof' in Freiburg, in the 'Hahnhof' in Köln and in Düsseldorf and in Hanover in the 'Hahnhof,' but this has never happened to us before, for eight years now we've been going everywhere to the 'Hahnhof,' but today is the last time we'll ever go to a 'Hahnhof,' that I can assure you!" The business manager was quite unconcerned, and with a hand gesture indicated to the waitress to collect the money. The man looked at the woman one more time and with the tip of his tongue moistened his lips which had become dry and cracked, and then merely said: "For a soup we didn't even eat!", but he spoke these words mostly to himself. The business manager bowed briefly but very correctly toward the two and also toward me and limped away, and the waitress pocketed the money for all four bowls, and the two rose and not until now, while they got up, did the hitherto sewed-up mouth of the woman burst, and she said—not exactly to the man, but rather into the universe, as it were—: "How could you possibly give in!" But he, visibly at the end of his strength, no longer felt the lash of her voice; he was presumably glad not to have to fight any longer, and passively let himself be led away.

A Case of Self-Conversion

He simply couldn't take it any more with her, and therefore he decided to get a divorce. She, however, was unwilling, and therefore there were new fights, more bitter than before; so he moved out of the apartment for the time being and sublet a place with friends. Soon everyone knew that he had had a falling out with his wife because he always talked about it and because he gathered witnesses for the trial who were to testify that his wife had neglected him, that she was lazy and wasteful and a drunkard and spiteful and cantankerous and not quite sane, and that she had made him ill with her unfounded jealousy and always had impeded his professional advancement and other similar things. People listened to him and said at first: "Let's hope things will work out." They spoke of similar crises with this or that couple; "oh, God, women," they philosophized. "Well, of course, that's no longer possible," said another; and others said: "You're quite right, she seems to have had it a bit too easy." Yet another perhaps ventured: "I would have put a stop to all that from the very beginning." Gradually they all agreed that divorce was the only solution; however, she was still unwilling, and he continued to talk about it with friends and with relatives and with colleagues. His father once said: "You were simply and fundamentally not compatible," and he replied: "No, not at all" and thought about it and while on vacation wrote to his father that it was still inexplicable to him since they had, after all, so many interests and views in common. After he had been separated from her for quite some time and she still had not agreed to his wish for divorce, a friend said: "You know, I think she wants to get you for as much as she can." He nodded very forcefully and then said: "No, I don't believe so. She's crazed about money, that's true, but she's surely not so shabby as to blackmail me." His brother-in-law, the husband of his older sister, told him: "It's pretty revealing that you still haven't moved out of that musty apartment of yours." He thought of the apartment he had left behind with its almost one-meter thick walls and with the deep window recesses and he thought of all the things that had gone on in this apartment in these few years and then said: "You know, we both were very fond of the apartment. It is gloomy, true, and not especially practical, but we were satisfied with it and felt at home in it with its coarse woolen curtains, with the pictures covering every free space of the wall, with the indirect lighting, a cozy nest. No, it was not the apartment." A pretty girl, whom he had drawn into his confidence earlier already, asked him: "I don't understand one thing: how a clever guy like you could fall prey to such a woman," and ever since he did not find her so pretty. From time to time he visited his lawyer, who said they would only win if they had truly weighty grounds; and as always he asked: "So, still no adultery?" And, since he came to hear the familiar negation: "Did she embezzle money? Did she refuse to move with you to another place? Were you never, in truth, assaulted and threatened? Grievously defamed with consequences for your career and profession?" And he told the lawyer that she was not a bad person, merely spoiled and perhaps pampered, but that he no longer could live with her. It was almost a year now that he had been living alone, and once it happened that someone congratulated him; but he told the man it was not at all a matter for laughing. The other replied: "I'm not laughing. I'm just thinking of what you are being spared: 'Don't smoke so much!' and 'Why don't you take the other necktie!' and 'Come and eat, will you!' and window-shopping and movies and once again window-shopping and whether the sandals match the handbag and the Mrs. So-and-so always checks the cash register receipts—one becomes crazy or a saint, a eunuch!" But he said: "We were friends. We were attuned to each other." The other one said, and they were almost arguing: "Until your nerves were frazzled." He said: "On the one hand you're right, of course, but actually you have a false impression: she is, you see, different from other women." She no longer visited his relatives and even less so their old friends, and everyone talked candidly about her: that she had drunk quite a bit and that she couldn't hold on to money; they spoke of dust in the curtains, of her spiteful tongue; he said: "No, words never failed her." And said: "She never drank during the day. Only in the evenings: with guests, at friends', in a restaurant. And she was the one who always drove when I—well, let's forget it!" And he said: "Women who always clean and sweep and wash and rinse—I have nothing but scorn for. Vacuum cleaning is cause for divorce." With the relatives, acquaintances and friends, who had agreed to testify, he mused: "Of course, jealousy is a sickness, a delusion. But can a woman, if she truly loves, really remain indifferent? No, she had definitely no cause, you know that. But," he continued to speculate, "is jealousy, as the fear of losing the beloved, is jealousy not the *conditio sine qua non* and therefore the proof of—well, of love? Is it not the price one has to pay? Love too has its price." He involved all those who wanted to testify on his behalf in endless discussions, in which he, to be sure, emerged the victor. He visited his lawyer only out of sheer habit. The lawyer said: "You talk and talk. And what does God do? He delivers us proof to our house!" And he reported: his legal assistant frequently plays tennis on the weekend on the Semmering, a drink at the bar in the evening, an inebriated braggart happens to be there, the woman not exactly sober either, the two in a room exactly opposite his, they should get together again sometime, "all drunks have the tragic impulse to get together again when they are sober," the lawyer said, and continued: "To be brief: My assistant catches the name and remembers, examines, as far as is possible, the dates in the guestbook, describes the woman to me, it turns out to be your wife. What do you say now?" He replied as coolly as if he had had to listen to an embarrassing joke: "That can happen." He listened to the lawyer talking and behind him, diagonally, he saw the rows of files, nothing else, only the senseless rows of files. He spoke diagonally past the lawyer, crossing his flow of words: "What's that compared to the other things, to all the other things!" And: "Forget it, please!" Then suddenly fully alert, as if in the midst of a discussion, he spoke directly to the lawyer: "There's only one thing I don't understand: why I did not return to her long ago." The lawyer knew, but did not say it.

An Unexpected Reunion

Actually she was not particularly fond of: welcome kisses, flirting and fondling, into bed, out of bed, and good-byes. She much preferred: talking of this and that, perhaps a record, Gilbert Bécaud or Mozart, showing off a new dress, wondering if it pleased him, and rummaging in old photographs, sharing an orange and more talking. She liked the way it was with him. What she had not liked with him, as often was the case, was his pontificating. Of course he was brighter than she, but she didn't want him to show it. "It makes me furious," she had shouted. "Thanks, I've had enough!" She had thrown him out and slammed the door and cut short the good-byes he had attempted. His behavior even then made him totally and ultimately intolerable. "Why the devil doesn't he shout back?" But the empty living room gave no response. She trudged with angular steps through the room and was annoyed that the carpet swallowed up her steps. Suddenly she turned on her heel, quickly pressed the knob on the television: any kind of noise would suffice. She squatted before the set, enjoyed its humming already, stared mesmerized at the bright screen and sipped her egg liqueur. The humming yielded to an almost comprehensible sound which articulated itself into a voice which was familiar to her, but which she did not recognize until he (she had just set down her glass) gradually came into focus: as if adjusted through a magnifying lens and no different than just before, here, in her room, leaning on his elbows, fingers clasped under his chin, supporting his face. His left eyebrow now raised, forehead wrinkled, the brow fell as he gazed upon the table as if into the manuscript, which he didn't even need. Then again the full gaze into her room. Into this gaze she hurled—jumping out of her chair—the glass with the egg liqueur. But the television screen remained intact and the egg liqueur was dripping stickily, hesitatingly, down from the hairline, streaking the temple, gumming up one eye, down upon the shoulder, veiling the mouth that continued to speak imperturbably, that continued to fill the room with words, just as before . . . . Hurriedly, as if afraid to be caught, and without the vaguest notion as to how she had seized the sponge so quickly, she wiped the screen: she exposed the mouth, nose and eyes, the forehead and the hair, dabbed the yellow liqueur from the jacket, cautiously polished the screen with her handkerchief, threw sponge and cloth into the sink, but when she returned, the face and voice of the announcer had come back: "You have seen a repeat of the tenth episode—" and she turned it off. There was an awkward silence in the room. She wanted to talk, yet she felt ridiculous as she made an attempt to talk to herself. Naturally it took her some time to lift the receiver and dial. She said: "Since you did ask, I do think that I would like it. I mean: to be married to you."

Lust and Lasciviousness of Monogamy

Since he was married and absolutely faithful he knew few other women; among them a likewise implicitly faithful one, with whom he now happened to be sitting one evening at a table in the dining car of the express train to Basel. They chatted, spoke about her husband, about business, about the divorce of his once already divorced brother, they sipped wine, she asked to borrow his Jacob Burckhardt, they talked about the definition of so-called marriage, of so-called fidelity; they were now standing outside in the passageway in front of her sleeping compartment, whitish train-station buildings flew past, he had said: "I couldn't do otherwise, even if I wanted to," and "Either one is notoriously faithful or not at all." She had told him of diverse admirers: with flowers, with ribaldry, with philosophy, one with money, all of them ridiculous. He said: "My wife virtually has to force me to take notice of a particularly attractive woman." Switching signals chattered into the railway car where the sleeping-car conductor had wished a good night long ago, bridges thundered beneath them, "Fidelity as constitution, not as morality." They did not merely skirt the issue but plunged into it, crisscrossed it, turning the topic from fidelity to infidelity, explored the reasons for adultery in order to salvage more clearly fidelity. An oncoming train roared past them, somewhat later the next one, which they no longer heard, inside the compartment, because everything within them was suddenly much louder: louder than any whirlpool, than any storm: clamor of myriads of men since time immemorial to all eternity. It was, afterwards, as if it could not have been: neither of them needed to confess anything at home.

Between the Lines

Everything that is happening at the moment is very important, but afterwards one is unsure how important it really was. Some things one writes down immediately and others not until they come up again. If one has written something, it strikes one as if it were no longer so important, and occasionally one believes that everything important is only important simply because it hasn't been written about yet. But one has written about chestnuts, bursting forth shiny and brown from their prickly hull, and still they are very important; that was along the railroad path in Enns, but the railroad path itself has never been written about. The train departed at five after seven, and if one still managed to catch it most of the time it was because the trains were almost always late at that time. The railroad path was already empty after one crossed the Bleicher brook, but if one turned around, one could detect in the far distance Erich P., who had failed school once or twice and no longer feared school as much as the others who still had something to lose. When the train could be heard rattling across the bridge he would run, if at all; had the train already left, there was another one at nine, and Erich P. always carried his playing cards with him. He was an outstanding swimmer, but after a fall from his bicycle he was left with a stiff elbow and therefore could get out of military duty; but he was unlucky and was ordered to Camp Mauthausen where he slipped insulin and other scarce remedies to the prisoners. He saved several dozens of them but surely not because he took a special liking to the prisoners. He simply did it out of habit; he too enjoyed being alive: later on, when he traveled around the country huckstering the felt slippers from his father's small factory, he soon came to know the best local tavern in every village with a shoe store. He liked to talk and he talked well about food, and then, when he turned forty and found a girl he liked but his parents did not, he committed suicide.

On the other hand, other things have been written: the Christmas packages from Aunt Beate, full of the truly valuable things like cogwheels from a broken watch and colorful glass bulbs and golden woven tassels of a curtain, and scraps, in general, from the table of adults. But one has never written about Alexander, when he looked toward the other end of the train station and said: "Look, Dad, there, the E-Locomotive, a 'Crocodile,'" and the reply was: "Oh no, it's only a 1020; the 'Crocodile' has eight axles and is much longer," and then, to avoid an argument, as one approaches and it turns out to be a "Crocodile," the 1089.03 after all and one says: "You were right, Xandi"; he was not quite four years old then. And also one has never written about what it means to have a father. One studied in Vienna and seldom had anything to eat, one cooked rice with two half onions and the cheapest tea from the large tin can from the grocer's across the street, and then one hit upon the idea of taking Engel's literary history to the antiquary. As a farewell one leafs through it, one more time, and happens to glance at German Classicism where the author is fully indignant: "Upon Goethe's return from Italy, *Don Carlos* was already completed; it is astonishing that Goethe failed to recognize at that time Schiller's genius." The word astonishing was underlined, and along the right margin in father's neat handwriting: "not to me." He had died when one was six and now one could not part with the book; it was lost later on, perhaps during a divorce. And that was never written, just as it was never written that one was simply too lazy later on to pay a visit to Aunt Beate, when she was deaf and blind and all alone having to wait to die.

But was all that truly important? And if it was: was it important not simply because it had never been written about? And: did one not write about things that were important simply because one did not wish for these things to stop being important? Was it for this reason that one never wrote about Erika's death, or because one could not find a word for her vanishing between the stroke and the death? One had visited her, and she was sitting in the second room by the window on a stool and was very small, not emaciated and shriveled, but small, simply scaled down, and she was surrounded by the room, larger than usual, as if empty already, and she said: "I did not realize how few friends one has." She had been, as a young woman already, the secretary of our Club, and at that time she had occasionally groaned and laughed, with raised brows and shoulders: "Oh, what shall I do with all my old men? Each one always wants to sleep with me." She sat on the stool and was very small, and she didn't have any money to go to the country for a few weeks.

One has written: how Glaser in front of the command post asks for a cigarette and is told: "Yes, just a minute," and then after five minutes, after one comes out, Glaser is dead. But one has not written about the one day of peace behind the front on the steep meadow, where down below was the sandy road and the deep ditch full of stench and slime and up above the low farmhouse stood and beneath the apple trees a brown and white spotted dog rolled down the slope with a giggling bark, while the record player, which no one probably was missing now in bombed-out Saint-Lô, could only croak forth from its His-Master's-Voice funnel "O sérénade près de Mexico" because there was no other record left; Betty Spell too with "Elle était swing" had been broken, and among the field-gray shirts and white laundry, which had been hung up to dry, suddenly stood a man in leather and said he was a pilot, shot down and bailed out, shot down from this sky, which suddenly no longer was as blue as before; the leather man got something to eat and to drink, he ate and drank and smoked like everyone else, and after he had gone, one knew that this day was not the real peace but nothing more than simply a day without shooting: the hollow vessel of reality, so to speak. One also did not write about the bedbugs in the military hospital, where later one lay amidst stench and plaster. The bedbugs were omnipresent, one could sooner dispel the air than the bedbugs. They were especially fond of sitting between metal and paper, and those were the splints along the limbs. They also liked the iron of the beds; they liked almost everything. What they did not like were the wounds; only maggots, not bedbugs, lived on blood; but in the room there were eight people and at least eight thousand bugs, and one could not quite explain to oneself what these eight thousand bugs were living on. One only sensed that they lived. There were so many that there was no room in the beds and under the plaster. Above every bed hung a little school slate on the wall, and even in the two little holes of the wooden frame which held the rope they sat, densely packed; and they also sat along the backs of books, which the wounded had asked for. Supposedly now and then there was a room free of bugs. There was some success if one placed the feet of the bed in cans filled with kerosene; but the bedbugs learned at once how to let themselves fall from the ceiling upon the beds. And ether, sprayed under the plaster, lasted only a few hours. And if there really was a room bug-free at one time, the next wounded person brought so many bugs along in his plaster cast that no ether was of any use nor any kerosene. Engelmann died, but the one with a gas burn kept his arm, and one patient, who had baffled even the great professor from Göttingen, was already groping six weeks later under the nurses' uniforms, and only the bedbug problem persisted. One of the patients who was able to hobble about brought some sturdy twigs from the garden, because with a fork one only tore the paper bandage between the plaster and the body, and one did not reach all the spots that were itching. One had only two cigarettes per day and one passed the time with killing bedbugs. Most could be killed at night, after the nurse was called and she turned on the light; only when it was dark did the bedbugs also crawl up the plaster on the outside and across the sheet and also on the naked skin; and when light was suddenly switched on, one could surprise them. Forty and fifty were killed per day and sometimes more, yet they did not decrease. That they did not decrease was long since known, and they were killed merely as a sport. One lived with them, and then after five months when the plaster cast was cut open on the side and unfolded like a shell and all the bedbugs escaped, blackening for seconds the white dressing table with their escape, one scarcely recognized oneself; and perhaps one had indeed become another in all this defenselessness, and perhaps therefore it was never written about.

Just as one has never written about women. Oh yes: one has written about Louise and also about Anna, but not about defenselessness. Always, whenever one is defenseless, one had said to oneself: this, precisely this, will be written. And precisely this never was written; at least not afterwards, at best beforehand, so that one had become quite skeptical oneself. Basically it was not much different from the bedbugs: there was no opportunity to defend oneself, and thus there comes a time when one stops asking oneself whether one will write this or not. Instead, one will go perhaps to the City Bar with Sigrid, to the sweetest bar in all of Vienna: Johannesgasse, two dozen steps from Kärntnerstrasse. The door is sometimes locked because the proprietor doesn't want any whores inside nor does he want moviegoers from the Kärntner-Kino; he only admits people who behave like people in Willi Forst films, because the bar looks as if it were the remaining footage from a Forst film. The bar is totally empty, even if guests are present: tables are standing only in front of the fauteuils along the walls, serving as a frame of a dance floor, polished by countless soles, where, however, no one is dancing anymore, just as no one is sitting down at the piano; an adjacent wooden cabinet disperses a few measures of Vivaldi followed by news, Laos perhaps and the budget, and no one is listening any more, one is all alone in the bar, where at each of the tables two people are sitting, who are making their declarations of love, which they otherwise never and nowhere would dare to make: "I'll always love you, Sigrid." Of course one does not say that; one only says: "It is the sweetest bar in all of Vienna." And perhaps one also says: "I should be at home sitting at my desk," and these words are more than one had actually intended to say. And Sigrid could now sit down at the piano: "When you say farewell, say softly 'Servus,'" she would know what's appropriate, but she does not sit down at the piano, but would much rather pull her knee to her chin and be seventeen, and suddenly one becomes nineteen, as one had never been nineteen, then, as a soldier in Normandy; and therefore, and nonetheless, one only says: "Have a look at these wall coverings! The entire world is worn and torn, only this silk is intact." She could reply: "Oh, well, here one notices that everything is much older than we ourselves," and she corrects herself at once: "Or much younger," but most likely she merely says: "Yes," and nothing else. And one says: "Everything is old already, but nothing is shabby yet." She says: "Everything is very pretty," but she did not say: "It's because of the dust. Everything here is covered with the shroud of dust, and that's why all the things are so well preserved." And actually one would simply like to explain to her that this is the place where one parts and is unable to do it, and then at best one says: "I like it when everything is solid and massive: the cover, as darkly colored as a carpet, on the piano there, and the floor lamp made of heavy brass, and the beams in the middle of the room, and all the rest. Do you like it, too?" And she likes it, and one studies once more the handwritten menu and also the slender beverage list, which is stuck in the thick metal base, and one has a drink and then leaves. And it is not until now that Sigrid asks, why is it that one does not sit at one's desk, after all: Why not? One is already wearing one's coat, and one only says: "One can go to the City Bar and one can sit at one's desk: one only needs to choose." One puts one's cap on. "And actually one has made the choice already." The door sticks for a moment. "And it's always the wrong one, whether this way or that." But outside Sigrid says: "I had a lovely evening with you."

And she was not told that the brown and white spotted dog with its giggling bark rolled down the slope because cider had been poured into its food; it was this cider, swiped from Pont Hébert, the bottles had been corked up, tied up and sealed with pale red wax, the people had gone to quite a great deal of trouble with the cider, that had made the brown and white spotted dog so drunk that he rolled down the slope with a giggling bark. And that too was never written. And one knows so much more now that has never been written and also all that which one will never dare to write. And therefore one will go with Sigrid to the City Bar, where the outside world, worn and torn, has been standing still for a lifetime and only the smoke from the pipe gathers and twirls in the cones of light from the low lights, and there, in the City Bar, one will tell her all this.

Yes, one will.

But: will one do it, or will one write it?

Afterword

Although Herbert Eisenreich's short stories deal with the sentimental and the tragic, the grotesque and the erotic, the author maintained that his central theme and subject matter is that of misunderstanding, misconstruing or misconception: a misunderstood gesture or misinterpreted action, an imprecise word that has unintended consequences. In his essay, "The Bad Example of Herbert Eisenreich," he claims that this motif of misunderstanding had its origin in his *Gymnasium* days in Linz, when his German teacher asked the students to expand on an anecdote from the diary of the nineteenth-century dramatist Friedrich Hebbel: A murderer is burying a dead man in the same spot where another person has buried a treasure. The murderer finds the treasure and takes it along; later, when the other person returns to claim his gold, he is mistaken as the murderer. Eisenreich admits not only that he had been immensely lazy at the time and never finished the assigned essay, but also that for the rest of his life he was concerned with this question of how to write such a story. He was haunted by the question of how anything was to be written. And so, human misunderstanding became his main theme.

Eisenreich's urban protagonists are anxious and alone, striving for love and happiness. But they talk past each other, live past one another, misunderstand their own lives. They are mentally inflexible, incapable of listening; they deny the past and fear the truth. They mistake physical attraction for emotional bonds, sexuality for love. The chasm between men and women ultimately becomes unbridgeable, the worlds too divergent. They are tied to preconceived notions and gossip and clichés; they attempt to escape reality through dreams or lies or repression; they are figures without orientation, who have lost the support of a stable world order. Enduring happiness and lasting human contact are unattainable. They live in a brittle, flawed reality, in an impenetrable modern world. A concatenation of misunderstandings is responsible for human sorrow.

Eisenreich, as a member of the postwar generation of writers, has read his Hemingway and Faulkner and is well-acquainted with the American short story. In his fatalistic, pessimistic world-view his protagonists exert no influence on the surrounding world but merely adapt themselves to events. Man's actual unhappiness lies in his reaction to his fate: unconditional acceptance of fate is the only solution. He should abandon ideologies or wishful thinking that do not correspond to factual events; mere chance or coincidences should be recognized as personal fate. Only then can man live "schicksalsgesund" (healthy in fate), a Doderer neologism which Eisenreich thoroughly admired.

Eisenreich, apolitical, rejected the political engagement in literature of a Heinrich Böll or a Günter Grass. Human suffering is not caused so much by social and political ills as by the human failure to understand and recognize. The loneliness and forlornness become an existential experience. Suffering and unhappiness result from man's lack of self-confidence, from a separation and dissociation from the transcendent order, from a disintegrating reality. His stories are fragmentary and open: he tries to capture a *moment* of love, of friendship, of growing up. With his compact, concentrated language he depicts fragments of reality, not a totality of existence. His protagonists move in limited spaces, in cafés, apartments, offices, where they encounter or recall first love, half-hearted affairs, love disillusioned by the monotony and triviality of daily life. These protagonists are not seen so much at work as observed during their free time, in bars, on trains, in hotels, in taxis; his characters are journalists and students, secretaries and accountants, lawyers and physicians; all are city people and most belong to the middle class. Only rarely do we come upon a specific name: usually Eisenreich writes only "the man" or "the woman" or "he" or "she"; this namelessness, too, emphasizes the anonymity of modern man, the anonymity of a city.

Eisenreich also rejected linguistic experiments. He was a conservative who believed in simple storytelling with precise and exact details and unpretentious, emotionless understatement. His cool and sober and ironic tone was considered reactionary in the 1970s and his aesthetic concepts largely ignored and repudiated by the younger Austrian writers. Nevertheless during his lifetime Eisenreich received numerous literary prizes including the Franz Kafka Literature Prize, the Austrian State Prize, the Anton Wildgans Prize, the Peter Altenberg Prize and the Medal of Honor of the City of Vienna. Eisenreich died in Vienna in 1986 at the age of 61. Although he lived and worked (as a freelance writer and foreign correspondent) in Hamburg and Stuttgart in the 1950s, he spent the last twenty years of his life in Upper Austria and Vienna. He was married and divorced four times. In addition to approximately one hundred short stories he also wrote essays, poetry, radio plays and novels. But it is the short story that remains his principal concern. He regarded it as the purest and most lyrical prose genre, telling of a momentary confrontation with life and love and death, a fragment of an unending narration.

Renate Latimer